MILES AND THE MAGIC FLUTE

HEIDI CULLINAN

When unemployed Miles Larson retreats to rural Minnesota to lick his wounds, his dissatisfaction turns him into prey for a powerful, ancient being. With an enchanted silver flute in his hand, Miles enters an erotic fairyland where the sorrows weighing on his heart don't exist at all. The catch to his newfound paradise: three different magical beings have their eye on his soul.

To escape the dreamworld, Miles must battle against the Lord of Dreams who wants a new slave, escape the mysterious beast who craves a bridegroom, and resist the sensual lures of the fairy Terris's charms. First, though, Miles has to overcome the bitterness in his heart that led him here in the first place. He must acknowledge that sometimes to find happiness, we must face our pain and sorrows—and for Miles, that's the most difficult challenge of all.

Heidi Cullinan, POB 425, Ames, Iowa 50010
Copyright © 2019 by Heidi Cullinan
Print ISBN: 978-1-945116-35-3

Cover by Kanaxa
Formatting by BB eBooks

First publication June 2010, Dreamspinner Press
Second Publication May 2014, Wilde City Press

www.heidicullinan.com

This one is for Libby Drew

Because her enthusiasm for the initial rambling
nonsense is the reason this really odd dream turned
into a novel.

Acknowledgements

Thanks to Hillari Hoerschelman, who is always there for the Spanish help, to Angela for Wiccan advice, to Dan, Cate, Signy, and Libby for beta reading, And thanks to my body, for teaching me the strange, twisted beauty and strength that can be found in pain.

Thanks also to my patrons for supporting me and helping produce this edition, especially Sarah Plunkett.

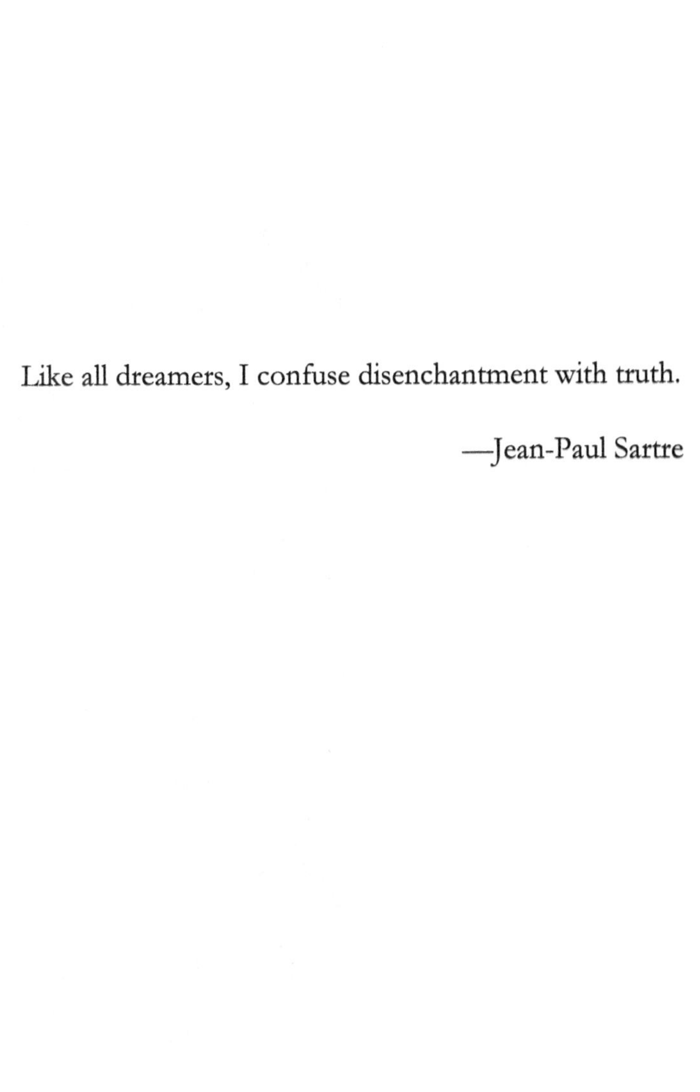

Like all dreamers, I confuse disenchantment with truth.

—Jean-Paul Sartre

CHAPTER ONE

Come faerie fair, come take me away.
Come take me to your hearth and stay
beside me in your glittering bower.
Take me faerie, and my heart devour.

MILES LARSON HUDDLED at his work table behind Patty's Pawn Plus, scraping black, horrid gunk off the tray of a toaster oven. He shoved the razor blade hard against the flimsy metal, swore, shoved again, and when the razor blade clattered from his frozen fingers, Miles gripped the appliance with all his humiliation, his rage, and his sorrow and thought, *I deserve so much better than this.*

An unseasonably bitter October wind whipped leaves around him, kicking a few into his face. Miles sighed and put the toaster oven down again.

The appliance was one Patty had salvaged from someone's trash, and she'd brought it to Miles at noon while he still lay in his bed. One minute, he'd been tucked beneath three layers of clothes and four layers of covers cursing Minnesota, cursing winter, cursing Fellerman Financial for laying him off and every other business in Atlanta for not hiring him, hating Jeff and his floozy, hating his friends who forgot about him the second he left town and didn't even bother to respond to any of his posts on Facebook—and then suddenly he had a lap full of toaster oven.

"Get up," Patty declared, "and fix this."

Patty's not even slightly passive aggressiveness drove Miles crazy. She didn't drop hints or even fight with you. She just told you what to do with enough butch power to make Diana Prince acquiesce. In contrast, Julie had knocked on his door, nudged him gently, suggesting maybe he could get up. She promised she'd have some breakfast for him, that she even had cow milk instead of soy milk, just like he liked. Julie had been in every half-hour since nine, cooing and coddling, trying to get Miles out of bed, into a shower, and back into his life.

Patty didn't roll that way. Patty hurled toaster ovens at you and shouted at you until you stopped moping and started working.

Miles now stood behind the shop, dressed in his long underwear and sweat pants and Patty's too-big parka, fumbling with frozen fingers as he tried to scrape the baked-on gunk away. He could go inside, and probably he should, but he couldn't bring himself to do so. For starters, there really wasn't room, and more to the point, he went crazy in there. He didn't know why exactly, but it probably had something to do with being surrounded by the detritus of other people's lives: the HDTVs and stereos and computers and MP3 players that people had purchased when times were better, goods that had ultimately been hocked, one at a time, to buy groceries and gas the car so the previous owners could go cash another unemployment check. It all hit a bit too close to the bone. So Miles worked outside, where his ego had space to explode, and where, when the cold dictated he had to stop and stuff his hands into his pockets to get feeling back into his fingers, he could stare off into the forest.

Miles loved this forest. If he were honest, it was the only part of Minnesota he'd missed while he'd been gone. When he'd grown up here, he'd lived on the other side of these woods on his parents' farm, and he'd cut through the narrow lip of the trees to Patty's dad's trailer to watch satellite TV pretty much every chance he could. His parents had moved to Minneapolis, and Patty's dad had gone to jail, but the woods had remained, and every now and again, Miles still snuck inside to reminisce. He wished he dared to do that now.

He fiddled with his phone instead, checking his mail and his messages on Facebook. There were none in either place. He scanned through page after page of people who had welcomed him at the bar, who had bought him a round and accepted his, of men he'd slept with and women he'd shopped with. He scrolled through the lives of his coworkers and his acquaintances, saw them laughing and kissing and teasing each other about the previous night out. They'd give him a quick note if he nudged them, but not once in six months had any of them instigated contact with him—not even the ones who were unemployed like himself.

Scrolling down a little farther in the feed, Miles saw a name highlighted at the beginning of a notification, and old habits made his heart flutter. Then he saw what the notification was, and his heart turned cold.

Jeff English is in a relationship.

Miles stared at the screen for a few seconds more. Then he tucked the phone back into his pocket, shoved his hands under his armpits, and walked up to the edge of the forest.

All the leaves had turned, and over half had fallen, leaving the place barren and still. Occasionally the wind would whip through, making the branches quiver and leaves rustle around in little eddies, but mostly the place was still and quiet and inviting. It was surely his fancy, but he felt as if the trees were beckoning to him, urging him to let go, to come inside. He couldn't do that, but he did give voice to a few metaphorical scrapings of the black sludge caked against his own heart.

"I hate this," he whispered to the forest. "I hate my life. I hate what I've become. I hate what I lost." He let the fury and the sorrow rise to the top of his throat. "I hate realizing that I never really had it."

The wind whipped up again as if in answer, and

Miles shut his eyes, letting it embrace him. For a moment, it seemed warm instead of cold, and when it pulled at him, drawing him forward, he didn't think—he simply stepped out, closing the distance between himself and the barrier of the trees.

If I keep walking, if I go into the forest, things will be better, a voice whispered in his mind. A feeling of peace stole over him, and Miles embraced it. *I can keep going and never come back.* In that moment, that was exactly what Miles wanted.

He took a step forward.

The back door to the shop opened, and the spell was broken.

"You about done?" Patty called. "I need you to watch the till until closing. Julie wants me to run into town for something for her soup."

Miles startled. He felt empty, as if something important had been taken away from him, and it made him angry.

"No, I am not about done." Miles stalked over to the toaster oven and picked up the razor blade, waving it angrily. "This shit won't come off no matter what I do to it." He gave the grime a particularly vicious swipe, but all it did was nearly cost him his thumb as the blade jumped the gunk and aimed itself at his other hand.

"Careful, now!" Patty scolded. "Nobody's going to buy that if you scrape the hell out of it."

It would have been so satisfying to throw the toaster oven against the wall, to watch the damn thing shatter into cheap metal and plastic bits. Instead, Miles settled for letting the tray clatter loudly onto the bench before tossing the blade after it, watching it skitter across the table.

"Fine," he said. "I'll do this later."

There was absolutely *no* satisfaction in receiving the glare that Patty gave him before ducking back inside the shop, and as Miles followed her through the towering shelves full of junk, he grudgingly admitted he deserved that, at least in theory. Whatever had gone on in his head at the edge of the forest had rattled him, but he had to push that aside now. He should be more gracious to Patty. She and Julie had taken him in when he had nowhere else to go, when he was bankrupt and sullen and friendless. She had given him a job and a roof over his head and a modicum of his self-respect back.

But Jesus H. Christ, did it have to be *this* job? *This* place?

I hate my life, Miles thought again, his hands clenching at his sides. *I hate my life, and I would do anything and give anything to change it.*

This time when the wind whipped up hard around him, it was so sharp that Miles paused, and on an impulse he couldn't name, he turned around and looked out at the forest. The pull of it was so strong that he swayed on his feet, and when the wind picked up again, it seemed to turn him and aim him at it, and

Miles went, not interested in fighting.

"Miles!" Patty shouted. "What are you doing?"

Blinking, Miles turned back around. "I—" He frowned, then shook his head to clear it. "I'm right behind you," he said, and followed Patty inside.

A HISPANIC FAMILY browsed as Miles came out to the counter, moving in quiet symphony, scanning the goods available with expert eyes, conversing occasionally with one another in Spanish. There were three men, four children, and one woman, but the woman was clearly in charge, because one of the men—had to be the husband—kept holding up items to her, asking, "¿Y ésta?" and she kept shaking her head. The other two men conferred quietly with one another over a selection of stereos.

Patty lectured Miles just out of earshot of the customers, with one eye on him and the other on the sales area. "Watch the store for me while I'm out. If you hear the bell, you have to come to the counter and stay until people leave. We don't normally have theft issues, but if you're not paying attention, that might change, because times are hard for everyone right now. Whenever there aren't customers, I need you fixing stuff. Toaster ovens, TVs, computers: whatever you can work your magic on. You're a real gift to us right now."

She made it sound like he was settling in for good. "I told you, I want to get a *job* again. Something in a *city*. Something in finance, not hobby repair. If this is about me earning my keep, I will absolutely pay you back. I appreciate your help, but this is not where I intend to end up in my life. This is just a temporary derailment."

Patty turned to him and put her hands on her hips. "Miles, you don't get it, do you? There *are* no jobs. You've been looking for months, and you've got nothing. Yes, this is about you earning your keep. It's also about you helping me. I don't want a guilt check six months from now. I want stuff I can use, and I want it now. I want your hands and your head. Nobody fixes stuff like you, Miles. You've got a real skill, and I want you to use it for me and for Julie. For yourself too. There's nothing wrong with your life, Miles. Just your attitude."

This rankled Miles, and he wanted to argue back, to tell her he was so getting a job. He wanted to tell her the fuck if he was going to stay here and repair toasters in the backwoods—but he didn't. He set his jaw and nodded curtly at her as he slid past her behind the counter.

He probably deserved the thin press of her lips that she gave him before grabbing her ski jacket and ducking out the door, making the bell above it jangle.

The family stayed in the shop for a solid twenty minutes, inspecting every item for sale at least twice, during which time Miles tried to watch them without looking like he was watching them. God, he hated this.

He was supposed to be in a sleek office building in Atlanta, buzzing his assistant to order a latte as he went over a prospectus. He was not supposed to be tucking his fingers into his armpits to keep them warm while he gave a stony glare that wasn't working to two jabbering children who were waving a hot pot around.

This is not the life I was meant to have, Miles thought, gritting his teeth and digging his fingernails into his sweatshirt. *I'm better than this. I deserve so much better than this.* The longing swept over him once again, and just as it had outside, for a second it burned in his chest, hot and angry and desperate.

A gust of wind blew up sharply against the pawn shop, rattling the cheap metal roof and sending a blast of draft through the single-paned window behind Miles. Outside the shop, the sheriff's German shepherds began to bark. Inside, one of the children stopped running around and looked warily at the front door. Miles looked too, trying to figure out what the little girl had seen, but nothing happened, and no one came in. The little girl whimpered, though, and ran over to her mother's pant leg.

"This," one of the men declared, setting a small CD player on the counter.

He pulled out his wallet and began peeling off bills, which was a relief to Miles. He hated when people tried to dicker over price when Patty wasn't around to demonstrate this was not an option. Miles rang him up and counted out his change, and as he handed it back, he happened to glance at the second man. The man buying the stereo was short and stout, but the man behind him was taller and leaner. He was also just a little bit handsome, and he smiled carefully at Miles. Miles smiled back, and he felt his blood kick up a bit too.

Then the darkness in his heart consumed him again, and he turned away. There was no time for flirting. He had to put all his focus on getting out of this dump.

Miles deliberately kept his gaze away from the man and forced a smile at the mother as she directed the purchase of a clock radio, a TV, and a popcorn popper. The children had calmed down, miraculously, though the young one kept repeating, "*¡Vamos!*" as she tried to urge her mother to the door. Miles watched them go.

Once the bell had stopped clanging and the shop was quiet again, Miles opened his eyes and looked around. There was no one in the place but him. Outside the dogs had quieted down, and the gravel crunched beneath the Mexican family's tires as they pulled away. But Miles felt listless, and he was cold, so he paced back and forth behind the counter, letting his mind wander.

Oddly enough, he found himself thinking of the forest most of the time. He remembered that strange warm wind and that feeling of peace. The quiet of the shop was heavy, pressing down on him like a weight. He wanted the close, sheltering feel of the trees, the expanse of space, the fairy-like feel of it. When he'd been young, he'd wished there were real fairies there, that they would come and play with him. In fact, sometimes he'd pretended they had. When he'd been in junior high and figured out his orientation, so incompatible with Summer Hill, he'd gone into the forest to do the crying he couldn't let his parents hear, and he'd wished, once again, for someone to take him away.

One day he'd thought the fairies had actually heard him, Miles remembered with a wry smile. He'd felt a breeze as if it were fingers touching his face, and he looked out into a nest of trees and swore he saw a shining castle in the clouds before a silver lake. That alone startled him, but when he heard what sounded like an animal moving through the woods, he'd gone back home. And actually, he hadn't gone back into the forest after that, not until he was in high school, but then he was just cutting through to visit Patty.

Miles wanted to go into the woods now. He felt restless and aching and full of longings no fling would fill. He wanted the ease of his old life back. He wanted that peace, the centering feeling reaching for his dream had given him. Patty might be right. That dream might be gone. But the forest was here. He could reach for the ease the forest had given him when he was young. Right now he wanted that peace so badly that he ached.

When five o'clock came and Miles shut down the shop, he didn't even pause to think, simply nipped around the back and headed for the woods. He felt the pressure build inside him and then release as he stepped over the border into the rustling leaves and dying undergrowth.

Miles smiled. Yes, he decided, this was what he needed. A brisk walk in crisp, October air through the woods of his youth. Just a short walk now, a short loop to say hello to the place again, but tomorrow he'd take a proper hike.

And if the fairies wanted to take him, they could damn well have him.

He'd meant the thought as a sort of joke, but he wasn't fifty feet into the trees before it didn't seem that funny anymore.

Something was wrong with the forest. Miles couldn't put his finger on what it was, exactly, and part of him was convinced he was just being ridiculous, but a bigger part of him could not let go of the idea that something was very, very wrong here. It looked okay— trees, brush, muddy path, dead leaves, flowers—but it was like those hidden pictures where there was a toothbrush drawn into the bark of a tree. Something was wrong, and his brain had him on high alert because of it. Miles stood there, frowning, trying to figure out what it was.

Then it hit him. He looked down at the ground, at the small patch of silver and green at his feet.

Flowers. Flowers did not grow in Minnesota forests in October, especially three days after a hard frost.

Miles crouched down and inspected the blooms

without touching them. He'd never seen flowers like them before. They reminded him of snowdrops, a flower which *could* bloom in Minnesota, but it generally didn't in October. It was a flower of early spring. He could see it coming up early if the weather were unseasonably warm, but it was quite the opposite. The weather this fall was cold, even for Minnesota.

Though, now that he thought about it, the forest was distinctly warmer than the area around the shop had been.

In fact, Miles wasn't shivering anymore, and he could almost feel his toes. The breeze against his face was warm and inviting. Very inviting.

Go deeper, it seemed to say. *Go deeper into the forest.*

Miles looked up, looked out across the barren landscape of dead leaves and dying underbrush, and he felt the pull.

Come. Come to me, lover.

The light changed. The yellow-pink light that ringed the edges of the trees didn't match the dull, blue-gray light he'd left when he'd shut the door to the shop, turning into the darker rose-purple sunset of summer instead of the gray into deeper gray of October. It absolutely was warmer here. Much, much warmer. Miles tried to tell himself that it was because the trees were close and blocked the wind, but something in his hindbrain insisted it was more than that. The air felt lighter. The foliage had been stunned by the same early frost that killed everything in southern

Minnesota, and above his head the leaves were well on their way to turned, some of them gone already. But it didn't smell like autumn, like rotting leaves and cold. It smelled of grass and sun and dirt. And it felt like summer.

Miles looked at the snowdrops again, frowning. It had to be his imagination. But it felt so real.

As he stared at the flowers, as the forest seemed to warm around him and confirm that he was losing his mind on top of everything else, Miles gave in to the despair that had been dogging him all morning. Instead of simply thinking it, he spoke the words out loud.

"I never thought this was where I was going to land at twenty-seven." He stared out into the woods, letting his eyes lose their focus. "I thought I'd have a good job and a killer apartment. I thought that I'd be looking at a promotion, not shoveling my way through job applications that don't get me anywhere. I thought I'd be adopting too many dogs with my boyfriend and planning vacations to Spain." He shut his eyes and felt the pain and hurt well up inside him. "I'm more than this. I don't belong here. I don't care if it's arrogant to think that way. I *don't*. And if I could find the way to get out of this miserable life and into the one where I belong, I would. Because I'm *so much better than this*."

Even with his eyes closed, he felt the light shift, which was why he opened his eyes just in time to see the rosy-purple fade entirely, replaced briefly with a deep, almost menacing indigo. For one second he could have sworn it was night, and suddenly his thirteen-year-old self's fear of this forest didn't seem so silly anymore.

Something deep inside Miles went cold and whispered, *danger.*

Heart beating hard inside his chest, Miles bent down and, without knowing why he did so, plucked one of the silver flowers.

A light flashed, bright and white and pure. He heard the voice.

Come to me. Come to me, Miles.

Miles felt a ghostly touch, warm but disembodied against his face. In the distance, he heard the sound of hooves.

Come to me and realize all your dreams.

Miles dropped the flower and ran.

He ran, pulse racing, cold now not just from temperature but from fear, and as he fled the forest, he told himself he was simply overwrought, that this was just his stress and depression getting the better of him, and he even admitted that it might be time to look into some medication and possibly some therapy. He couldn't help, though, turning and looking back as soon as he was into the trailer park again, trying to reassure himself.

The colors of the forest had faded back to normal, and the silver flowers were gone. But before Miles could sigh in relief, he saw that a single flower remained, and as he watched, its petals drifted eerily up into the sky, only to be carried away on an eddy of the wind.

A silvery ghost-like form appeared near the place Miles had been standing. It smiled sadly at him.

Miles gasped. Then he reached for it.

The ghost form faded, and the forest was normal once more.

Miles stood there a moment, hand still outstretched, feeling foolish and confused. Shaking his head, he lowered his arm and went back to Patty's trailer.

CHAPTER TWO

Come, lover, my sweetest heart and mind,
come take me to the place your kind
spends every day in languish deep.
Take me to the darkest keep.

MILES DID HIS best to forget about whatever it was that had happened to him in the forest, and when nothing else weird occurred for the next few days, he began to relax. He kept a wide berth of the trees just to be sure, but he began to forget about the strange happenings in the woods and soon went back to actively hating his life. He did notice, though, that he seemed more testy than usual. Prior to his woodland encounter, he'd been moody and depressed, but now he was moody and angry. He was listless, even more so than usual, and it made him edgy. He'd never been exactly tolerant, but he found himself angry at slow drivers on the road and pretty much all the clerks at the Walmart. He told himself that it was because all his job applications had come back as rejections again. He told himself it was because Jeff had sent him a drunken text letting him know how hot his new boyfriend was, and when Miles hadn't responded, Jeff had followed up with a photo.

Yes. Jeff's new boyfriend was exceptionally hot. Goddamn it.

Except he couldn't attribute his unease to Jeff alone. Miles's dreams were strange, too. He was always running through the forest, calling for someone he could never find. Sometimes he woke within the dream, and when he sat up in bed, the figure from the forest sat at the foot of it, studying him. But when Miles reached for the ghost, he would vanish, and Miles would open his eyes for real and find he'd been in a dream within a dream.

He dreamed the man and the forest over and over and over.

Then there was his run-in with Katie.

For a town of less than a thousand people, Summer Hill was ridiculously awash in lesbians. It had been that way even when Miles was in high school, so much so that rival teams (and sometimes even the local one) nicknamed Summer Hill "Dyke Stop." In addition to Patty and Julie, there was an older couple in town, the head librarian, and Miles had deep suspicions about the county attorney. But there was also Katie, Summer Hill's resident witch.

Wiccan, she would correct Miles every time he called her a witch, which he did largely to annoy her. It wasn't that Miles minded so much that she was Wiccan, and obviously he didn't care about the lesbian part. It was the Katie part that drove him crazy. She was always so damn superior about everything, always giving Miles a knowing look that managed to unnerve and belittle him all at once. He'd taken great pleasure in pointing out his successes to her when he'd come back to visit on occasion from Atlanta, largely because she'd spent most of their high school years promising him woe and doom whenever she read his fortune. It was, of course, a very bitter pill to be back here now, full of the woe and doom she promised. He avoided her and her pitying looks as much as possible.

But Julie was a budding practitioner of the Craft herself, and Miles was often called on to run over to the shop Katie kept in the back of her house for this or that herb or colored candle. She always had something special just for Miles, too, some scathing remark or portent of further misery which served as an opening act to her offering to read his cards, make a charm, or balance his chakra. Miles never took her up on any of it, just stood as close to the door as possible with his arms folded, waiting for her to stop needling and fill Julie's order so he could get the hell out of there.

The Friday after he'd felt the weird presence in the forest was no exception. He came through the back door, tensing as she put down the book she'd been reading behind the cash register and came toward him, silken caftan fluttering around her ample form as she clucked and cooed.

"Oh, poor Miles. You look so tired. Shall I put on a pot for tea while you wait? I can make you a restorative." She clucked her tongue as she ran her eyes up and down his body and shook her head. "Oh, dear."

All that was pretty much the usual, and Miles ignored it as he always did. But then she looked at him again.

She stopped, startled. A real startle, not the fake one she usually gave, which Miles knew was just to get his goat. He watched out of the corner of his eye as she frowned, and the gesture was so unsettling he couldn't help but bite.

"What? Why are you looking at me like that?"

But she didn't answer, which was even odder still. She went back to the counter, though she glanced occasionally back at Miles, unnerved. "What is it Julie needs?"

"I have a list." Miles dug it out of his pocket, and when Katie didn't take it from him, he laid it on a nearby table. She came back over—carefully—picked it up, gave it a curt nod, then busied about the shop, pulling down jars and opening up little plastic baggies. She didn't say another word to Miles, but when she glanced at him, she bit her lip again.

Suspecting a joke, Miles held himself rigid, determined not to give in, but the rage built inside him, and it wasn't even two minutes before he blurted out with a sharp sneer, "What the fuck is it, Katie?"

His tone was so harsh he even surprised himself. Katie, however, only put down the silver scoop and turned to Miles, quietly thoughtful.

"How long have you been like this?" she asked.

"Like what?" Miles snapped.

"Angry," Katie replied. "Your aura is so spiky it's cutting across the room, breaking down several spells I cast around the door to ward off just such a thing. You're rending them like spider webs." She tilted her head to the side. "When did this start? Because I'm getting the feeling this burst of temper isn't just for my benefit."

A snippy denial leapt to the tip of Miles's tongue, but the heat of it surprised even him, and as the pique bounced back against Katie's calm, he found himself gentling.

He took a step farther backward toward the door and leaned against it. "A few days ago." He didn't like the look she was giving him, the witchy assessing one, so he added, "It was just after I got another rejection letter for a job. It's nothing. Don't even think of trying any spells on me."

He braced himself, because this was where she would cajole and tease and lecture him about his energy and the need for balance. It was when he would throw her weakness for refined sugar back at her, and soon they'd be lobbing insults back and forth like they were balls and there was a tennis net between them. He was even looking forward to it.

But she only held up her hands and said, "I wouldn't dream of it." She grimaced at the air around him one last time, then tucked her hands inside her sleeves and nodded curtly. "I'll just get the rest from the back," she said, and disappeared behind the beaded curtain that led to her storeroom.

Miles remained in the doorway, confused.

The rage simmered inside him, lava looking for an outlet. He thought of what Katie had said about the spells he had rent, and even though he didn't believe in any of that stuff, Katie did, and she was clearly upset, which began to make him feel uneasy too. He really did think this was all just an overdue therapy appointment ricocheting around inside him, but as he stood there, blood boiling, it was easy to believe it was something more as well. He could almost feel the strings around his heart, binding him, stirring him, rousing him, and in his fancy, he imagined they extended all the way through the door, down the road and back down the valley, up and over all the way to the forest. The tug increased, and Miles shut his eyes as it pulled him flush against the door.

Come. Come, lover. Come, a soft voice whispered. *I can make all the rage, all the pain, all this sorrow go away.*

Miles's body purred in response, his rage rolling over and becoming, to his surprise, a low-grade lust. *Yes*, he thought, and fumbled for the doorknob. *Yes. Yes, hold on, I'm coming—*

But his fingers missed the door, landing on a shelf

beside it instead, and he stilled as his fingers touched something cold and smooth. The tug stopped at once, and when Miles looked down he saw a small silver ring quivering beneath his fingers. And as he continued to touch it, the rage continued to bleed away, not entirely but enough to make him realize that he had been about to go out the door and run to the woods.

He picked up the ring and stared at it, foreboding sliding like ice through his veins.

This moodiness was more than just being out of joint over not finding a job. This was more, even, than being back in Summer Hill.

Miles pinched the ring between his fingers. Something was going on. Something really weird.

Something possibly dangerous.

When Katie came back through the beaded curtain, Miles started, and barely realizing he did so, put the ring inside his pocket.

"Here you go," Katie said, putting a small parcel inside the cloth bag where she had placed the rest of Julie's order. "Tell her I'll just put it on her tab." She brought the bag over and set it down on the table where Miles had placed his list. Then she paused, and almost in afterthought glanced over to the shelf where the silver ring had been.

Miles tensed.

A cold wind whipped through the shop, putting out the candle Katie had been burning at the register.

Katie drew back, her face carefully blank. "Have a

good day, Miles. Give Katie my best. And tell her not to perform that consecration until the full moon."

Miles nodded gruffly and reached for the bag. He flushed, and then, because he couldn't seem to bring himself to pull out the ring, reached for his wallet and pulled out a twenty instead. But Katie held up her hand to stay him and shook her head.

"Keep it," she said quietly.

She sounded afraid.

Miles swallowed, stuffed the twenty back into his pocket, and turned away.

"Take care, Miles," she said, her voice ominous and a little sad.

Miles yanked the door open. A cold wind buffeted him, but he pushed past it and stormed all the way to his car and drove in silence back to the trailer. After parking the car, he sat and stared out the window for a few minutes, not sure why he did so. He stared out through the trees toward the forest, and it made him feel good and quiet and calm.

Come, Miles. Come to me now.

Yes, Miles thought, and opened the car door, ready to run for the woods. But when he stood, he heard something clink against the pavement, and when he looked down he saw the silver ring. When he put it on, the urge to run into the forest vanished. His rage, however, remained, leashed but still there, banked and waiting.

It stayed that way for days.

He never, not even in the shower, took the silver ring off his finger.

Somehow Miles knew this was not over, whatever it was. Because sometimes late at night, he could feel the forest pulling on him again, despite the ring. It kept trying, and it kept getting stronger, and he lay awake most nights in a quiet panic, trying to decide whether this really was the work of some supernatural force or if he were just losing his mind.

Then the flute showed up at the pawn shop, and he didn't know what to think about anything after that.

MILES HAD BEEN working in the shop alone when it came. The door had opened right after he'd stapled his sleeve to the supply shelf as he tried to re-hang, with some irony, the sign that warned, "Not Responsible For Accidents." Doing his best to turn around with his arm affixed above his head, Miles smiled in the general direction of the door.

"Can I help—" He saw who had just walked in, and his smile died. "Oh, fuck," he said, and tugged with some urgency at his sweater. Warren Lehman stood in the doorway of the shop, leering.

Warren was the author of at least fully half of Miles's neuroses, beginning when Miles was twelve and Warren's gang of thugs had pushed Miles's face over a used toilet bowl and threatened to make him drink the water if he hadn't said, like a good little parrot, whatever humiliating line they had arranged for him that day. "I'm a stupid little faggot fairy queen" had always been a fan favorite. He'd soon learned to curb his intake of fluids and developed a bladder of steel, and by the time he'd turned fifteen, he'd met Patty and none of that mattered because Patty kicked everyone's ass, sometimes just because she wanted to. Eventually Warren had been permanently suspended from school and gone to juvy for lighting a freshman on fire, and then all Miles had needed to do was avoid dark alleys until he went to college.

But Warren was a memory that lingered, and now he was here, grinning a devil's grin around the wad of what was undoubtedly chewing tobacco in his mouth. Miles, still trapped by the staples in his sleeve, felt panic rise.

"Well, I'll be damned if it isn't Miles Larson, come home to Summer Hill with his tail between his legs." Warren tossed a sneer to Daryl and Ham, his sidekicks from school days and apparently now as well. "Should have figured the fag would come work for the dykes."

The tone was just right, and so was the pitch, and he even had the gang of thugs with him again. The primal memories rose up almost as a Pavlovian response, and Miles cowered.

And then, like someone had flipped a switch, rage swept through Miles hot and sharp. He turned, ripping his sweater loose. He didn't even pause when the gesture put a hole in it—he only stalked up to the edge of the counter and pressed his palms against the edge of it so he could glare at the thug right in the eye.

Warren took a step backward, his eyes wide and full of surprise.

Miles grinned a nasty grin and tightened his hands into fists.

The gesture made his thumb brush against the circle of the silver ring he'd stolen from Katie, and Miles's mental switch flipped back, the rage retreating to a simmer again.

He lifted his chin to give Warren his most brittle smile. "Warren. What can I do for you?"

Daryl and Ham had cardboard boxes in their arms, and at Warren's nod, they put the containers on the counter that stood between them and Miles.

"Came to pawn my shit, dumbass." Warren nudged the one he'd put down and gave Miles a curt nod. "And you're giving me top dollar, you little cocksucker, or I'll beat the living crap out of you."

Ten years. It had been ten years since high school, and Miles had done a lot in that decade. He'd been a team leader in his department, and if they'd called him back from his layoff, he would have stepped right back on track for his shot at junior VP. He couldn't even remember the last time someone had threatened him with physical violence, and he was pretty sure that when they had, he'd just ignored them and kept walking. Now here he was back home, and Warren Fucking Lehman only had to look at him sideways and he was fourteen again, afraid of being hung up over the post of the bathroom stall by his underwear again.

And just like that the rage was back. Cower to Warren Lehman? Fuck *that*.

This time Miles very carefully kept his thumb from touching the ring as he gave Warren another saccharine smile. "It's so good to see you haven't lost your small town charm. By the way, how's work going?"

Warren glowered. "I'm laid off, fucker, just like everybody else."

Miles nodded in empathy he absolutely didn't feel. "That's too bad." His heart pounded, though, and he felt as if he were split in half, part of him trying to scramble to safety while the other stepped boldly into harm's way. The ring pulsed gently now, but so did the rage. Miles picked at the threads the staple left on the edge of the hole in his sweater and cleared his throat, trying to collect himself.

"I'm sure you'll find something eventually." He tossed the threads he'd pulled out into the trash, shoved up his sleeves, and approached the boxes. "Let's see what you have."

What Warren had, of course, was pretty much junk, and even as much as Miles hated him, it was sobering to see what Warren had of worth to sell from his miserable little life. Four CDs, two Blu-ray boxed sets, a Blu-ray player, an outdated cell phone, a portable stereo, a toaster, and a percolating coffee pot. Miles was still learning this gig, but he was already pretty sure

Warren was looking at twenty bucks, tops, and that was only if Miles was feeling generous. Which he wasn't.

Warren, who apparently knew this, too, tightened his hand into a fist and rested it on the edge of the box as Miles peered into it.

"Hmm," Miles said, buying himself some time. He had a few words with his angry self, pointing out that if Warren hit him he'd get charged for assault, but Miles would still end up with a busted face. The rage wasn't much moved, and the next thing Miles knew, he'd pasted on the false smile again. "I can take the electronics, but Patty doesn't do CDs or Blu-ray. Try eBay." He scanned the lot once more, then kept the smile in place as he said, "Fifteen."

Warren slammed his fist on the counter so hard even Daryl and Ham jumped. "You little *faggot.*"

Inside Miles panicked, but the rage still drove, and it leaned forward, grinned terribly, and whispered, *Yes.*

Behind Miles, a door slammed into the wall. "Is there a problem?"

Miles didn't know how Patty did it. She was big, but she wasn't tall, and honestly, as a woman, she should have been instantly dismissed by someone like Warren, *especially* when he had Dumb and Dumber as backup. But Warren didn't dismiss her. In fact, he backed up and toned down quite a bit just at the sight of her. It calmed the beast inside Miles, too, leaving him with mental space enough to feel queasy at the thought of how close he'd come to becoming a greasy streak against the wall.

No one paid any attention to him now, though. This was a stand-off between Warren and Patty.

"This stuff's worth more than fifteen dollars," Warren said, still angry, but less aggressive about it. He gestured to his boxes, then to Miles.

Patty came forward and peered into the boxes before giving Warren a very heavy look. "Miles was being generous. I would have quoted you ten." When Warren made more noise, she raised a finger at him. "Listen here, buddy. I buy what I can resell. Everybody here is in the same shit you are, which means I am up to my eyeballs in everybody's useless garbage they should be putting on garage sales. You can take ten dollars right now and say thank you to me and sorry to Miles, or you can pick up your goddamned boxes and get out. Because my taking your shit for ten dollars is a *favor*. If you don't act appropriately, the favor is rescinded. Understand?"

Warren was red-faced and furious, but it was also clear he knew he was beaten. But rather than agree to the ten, Warren reached into the box farthest from him and pulled out a small black case, a case Miles realized he'd overlooked as part of a DVD box set.

"This has got to be worth more than ten."

Patty took the box from him and opened it, and Miles gasped.

It was a flute. A very small flute made of what was very possibly silver. It didn't look like most flutes Miles had seen, and he should know, since he'd played one in high school. This flute was all one piece, looking almost like a piccolo, but it was longer, and it had no covers for the holes or any levers of any kind. There was etching in the metal, delicate swirls and whorls, and some writing that reminded Miles of Elvish in the *Lord of the Rings* movies.

He could have sworn the light shifted in the pawn shop the second Patty opened the case.

Patty took the flute out carefully from the velvet lining and weighed it in her hand. "You steal this, did you?"

"It was my grandma's, or something." When Patty just raised an eyebrow, Warren added indignantly, "I found it in a box in the attic."

Miles would have laid good money that the flute was stolen. At any rate, he was pretty sure Warren's grandmother had been dead fifteen years.

"Hmm." Patty turned the flute over a few times, rubbing her finger across the holes, inspecting the ends. Then she put it back into the box and closed it with a snap. "Fifty. For the lot."

Miles suspected Warren would have fought this price earlier, but after nearly walking out with only a ten spot, he let out a sigh of relief and held out his hand. But when Patty opened the register, she pulled out a pair of twenties and a five. When Warren opened his mouth to object, she gave him a feral smile and braced both hands on the counter, trapping his money in her palm as she leaned closer to address him.

"Haven't you heard about my policy, Warren? I counted five slurs out of your mouth once you came through the door, four aimed at Miles and one at Julie and me. That's a dollar each. Outfront Minnesota thanks you for your generous contribution to their effort to bring marriage equality to our state and further the rights of LGBT persons." She held out the money, her smile turning sweet. "And you have a *very* nice day."

Warren snatched up the money with a glare and nodded at Daryl to pick up the box of DVDs & CDs. "Bitch," he murmured, but under his breath as he led his sorry little posse back out the door.

Miles watched them go. "Aren't you worried they'll retaliate in some way?"

"The county sheriff is next door, and Julie keeps him neck-deep in baked goods. Anybody messes with the lesbians who run Patty's Pawn Plus will shortly get a visit from the law, and that's a fact well-known in Summer Hill and several neighboring communities. Plus, Warren knows damn well I can aim my gun and reload faster than his fat little fingers can manage. Though that protection won't automatically extend to you, so I'd stay out of shadowy alleys and parking lots." She picked up the box that held the flute and handed it to Miles. "But first do some research on this for me. I have the feeling we just made one hell of a deal, but I don't know where to sell a flute."

Miles watched Patty pick up the boxes, noting the way her biceps bulged as she lifted them. Patty was the butchiest butch he'd ever met. She was short, but she was stocky, and her features and build were so mannish that *he* almost found her attractive. He didn't like the tattoos, though, that snaked around her shoulders and down both arms. She did, and so did Julie, which was probably why Patty was wearing a tank top even though it was so cold in the shop that Miles was considering putting on gloves.

Except it wasn't cold now, Miles noted. He'd been freezing before Warren came in, but now he was quite warm. Maybe it was from being so angry? Miles looked down at the flute, still open in its case. When he looked at it, the feeling of warmth increased. And when he touched the metal, he could have sworn he smelled summer. The ring on his finger had warmed, too, and the rage was entirely gone now. He felt good, really good.

He felt the phantom brush his cheek again, and he snapped the box shut.

"I'll have to go back to the trailer to research," Miles said.

"That's fine," Patty said, picking up another box. "I'll call over if we get busy."

The cold had come back, and Miles shivered. He looked down at the black box in his hand and frowned. It was just like the forest again, except this time he wasn't in the forest. Was whatever this was following him around?

God, did he actually just ask himself that?

"Patty," he said at last, "how do you know if you're going crazy?"

"You're not crazy," she said matter-of-factly and thumped her box down. "Just neurotic and sulky. You've always been that way."

Miles sagged. "I just don't feel very stable. I keep seeing things. *Smelling* things."

"You've been out of work for six months. Your boyfriend is dating a muscle-bound hottie he met in a bar. You're bankrupt and friendless and living back in the shit town you grew up in, holing up in my double-wide and working in my redneck pawn shop. You're a snotty, proud bastard, and right now life is rubbing your nose in the shit. If you *weren't* seeing and smelling things, I'd worry." She clapped a hand on his shoulder and nodded at the door. "Now go make me some money on that flute. And don't let Julie turn the heat up over sixty-five."

Feeling somehow even more frustrated after Patty's rational dismissal, Miles tucked the flute against his side and headed for the door. A cold, biting wind met him there, no trace of summer at all. The tinkling sound he heard wasn't magical, just the bell above the door.

The fact that it followed him all the way back down the road until he reached the trailer park must have been his sullen, pouty, snotty imagination.

PATTY AND JULIE lived in a double-wide trailer in the trailer park behind the pawn shop. It was the same trailer Patty had grown up in, back when the pawn shop had been her dad's, but it was a lot nicer now than it had been when Miles visited Patty during high school. The outside was still a dingy gray, but the inside was clean and sparkling. That was because of Julie.

Julie was everything in a woman that Patty wasn't. She was slight and tall and shockingly beautiful, a state only heightened by the fact that she never wore any makeup whatsoever. Julie was absolutely granola: she kept a garden in the lot beside the shop, and she spent the whole summer either weeding or canning. She traded her vegetables for wool from local farmers, which she spun into yarn, then dyed and either sold it at local farmers' markets or on the Internet. She cooked, she knitted, and she raised chickens, even though she herself was vegan.

She was in the kitchen when Miles opened the door to the trailer, bent over a pot at the stove, her shining blonde ponytail limp and curling from the steam as she wiped a hand absently on her blue-checked apron. This lovely domestic image was ruined, however, by the fact that the whole trailer reeked of a manky, sour smell that Miles couldn't place and frankly didn't want to. He gagged, pinched his nose, and tried in vain to find a space in the room that wasn't clogged with the stench.

Julie frowned in apology. "It's the dye," she said, still stirring the pot with a wooden spoon. "I'm staining some yarn, and if it turns out well, I'm going to sell it on Etsy. Just another half hour and I'll be all done."

Miles kept his nose pinched as he hurried around the table toward the narrow hallway. "Just going back to my room," he said.

Julie put down her spoon and turned toward him. "Miles, before you go, I need you to look at my food processor for me. It isn't working right, and I need it to mince some garlic for hummus I want to sell at the co-op."

"I'll look at it later." Miles ran down the hall and shut the door behind him.

He could still smell the dye, though, and he ended up having to open a window to get rid of it, which meant that he was even colder here than he'd been in the pawn shop. Grumbling, he fished in his drawer for a second pair of socks, donned a sweatshirt and wrapped his comforter around himself at the desk as he settled in at the computer.

He didn't even know where to start. He googled "flute," which buried him in worthless nonsense. He went to eBay and checked their prices, but the only things selling were regular modern flutes. He tried "flute collectors" and got a few interesting possibilities. Noting the emails and bookmarking the pages, he continued his scan, thinking he should try looking for some auction sites, too, both for musical instruments and for antiques. It looked like he might be able to get a couple hundred dollars for it, which would make

Patty very happy—though to sell it, of course, she'd have to either give more money to Warren to buy it outright or wait a month before he came back to get it. Except something in him felt like it should be worth even more. If it were real silver, the metal alone should be worth that, shouldn't it? He wished he knew what questions to ask.

Frowning, Miles's thumb rubbed against the silver ring, letting it soothe him while he considered his approach.

In the end, Miles emailed a few of the collectors, describing the flute in detail. He also took a few photos of it and attached them to his emails, figuring the gesture couldn't hurt. He checked eBay again, making sure he'd exhausted all the categories, then closed the browser, ready to take a break on social media. But as he moved his cursor to his bookmarks bar, he caught himself whistling, and he remembered the weird light and the bells and the way the shop had seemed to warm.

He paused, and then on the premise that googling never hurt anybody, typed, "magic flute."

He got over one million hits, all of them having to do with Mozart's opera.

Miles rolled his eyes at himself, but he grinned too. *No such thing as magic in Minnesota.* He drove the point home by scrolling through page after page of search results, each one more mundane than the one before. On the seventh page, he saw a link to "Terris's Faerie

Realm" with the preview listing necklaces and silver charms for sale, and he felt bold enough to click through, thinking surely the lineup of Wiccan baubles would chase away the last of his paranoid visions of things that haunted him in the woods.

But when he clicked the page, it was black. The whole screen was black, in fact, except for the menu bar.

Miles waited several seconds for the site to load, but nothing ever happened. Frowning, he hit the back button to try again.

Nothing happened. The browser stayed where it was, neither loading nor returning to the search page. When Miles tried to close the application, it was frozen. His mouse could move fine, but he couldn't select anything.

"Come on." Miles clicked the mouse three times in angry succession.

The whole room went black.

CHAPTER THREE

For in that place, I know the way—
there is one to save and one to slay.
One to kill and one to play.
And one Lord o'er all to make them stay.

MILES LET OUT his breath in a soft gasp. It seemed to echo in a way that didn't fit the room. His tiny bedroom was also an office, and outside of the bed, desk, dresser, and shelving there was about three square feet of available space in the center of the room, most of that taken up by the office chair. And yet from the way his breath echoed and by the simple feel of the space around him, Miles would have sworn he was in a large, high-ceilinged room, empty of furniture and likely lined with marble. He was still seated at his desk, and he had the mouse in his hand, but he was fairly sure the desk was somehow no longer in his bedroom. And neither was he.

It was cold too. Yes, he had the window open, but there wasn't a breeze any longer. The air didn't move at all. This was a different cold. Deep cold, like the bottom of a cave. Cold like winter. Miles couldn't smell Julie's dye any longer, but he was definitely smelling something. Something… off. Manky. Damp, dirty, and maybe even furry. It smelled like a basement, but it smelled like a basement where several unfortunate animals had died a long time ago.

Miles heard something else, something more than his own breathing and the quiet hum of the computer. Something soft and distant. *Click. Click. Click.* The snap of women's heels on tile, except these were no points of stilettos. They were heavy points. *Click, click, click,* and behind that, something dragging.

From not very far away, Miles heard a snort and a huff, like an animal.

Hooves. Hooves could make that heavy clicking sound.

And something dead killed by something with hooves could be the dragging.

Terror whipped up inside Miles, and he deliberately did not breathe.

He might have stayed there forever, frozen in terror, but eventually he began to notice an odd sensation on his left hand where he wore the silver ring. At first it seemed to pinch, and then it itched, and then it became warm, and then warmer, and then warmer still, and then Miles let go of the mouse and tugged on it, gasping in pain as he tried to get it off his finger. When he succeeded, he cried out in relief, then despair as he felt it fall from his fingers and clatter loudly on what sounded like a stone floor.

Across the room, Miles heard the huffing sound again, followed by a low, angry growl.

Heart pounding, Miles fumbled for the mouse, moving it quickly but carefully across the surface of the desk.

The mouse went *click*.

The light came back.

Miles was in the office again.

He was sitting at the computer, the familiar room all around him, just like it had always been there. Except Miles's mouse hand shook. Sweat rolled down his cheeks, and he didn't move until the sharp breeze kicked in through the window. In a trance, he rose and shut it, then stood gripping the sill for several seconds. When the computer made another soft *click* behind him, he jumped as if it were a gunshot, but when he dared to look, he saw that it had simply shifted into screensaver mode. Cheerful photos of Julie and her baked goods faded in and out of the screen.

You're tired. You hardly slept last night. You're emotionally drained. You probably read a book like this recently, or saw a movie. The excuses made so much sense, and they should have been comforting. They were, too, until Miles took a deep breath to center himself. And that's when he realized that something was really, *really* wrong.

He still couldn't smell the dye. The dye smelled sharp and sour, like vegetables and vinegar, which, knowing Julie, was exactly what it was. He couldn't smell it at all.

But the stench from the cave was stronger than ever.

Miles made no conscious decision to leave the room. One second he stood there freaking out, and the next he was in the hall, bolting for the kitchen. He skidded around the corner, slammed into the broom cupboard, then clung to the door as if at any moment a great wind might whip up and take him away.

"Miles!" Julie put down her wooden spoon and hurried over. "What happened? You're white as a sheet!"

Miles didn't even know how to begin. "I don't know, but I think I'm hallucinating."

Julie gave him a sharp look. "Did you take anything?"

He realized she meant drugs. "No!" he said angrily. He rubbed the side of his face. "I think I'm just stressed." He winced as his ring finger began to throb, and when he looked down he saw an angry red circle where the silver ring had been.

"You hurt yourself," Julie said, pointing to his finger, and reached for the first aid kit. "Here," she said, handing it to him, then headed to the refrigerator. "Put some salve on that, and I'll make you a protein shake." She hauled several jugs and containers out of the fridge and set them beside the blender. "And then I'll do your cards too." She frowned and nodded at his other hand.

"What's that?"

Miles looked down. He was holding the flute case in his right hand. Funny, he didn't remember picking it up.

"Something somebody brought in to the pawn shop this morning." He set it down carefully on the table before sitting in the chair farthest from it. "I was researching it for Patty on the Internet, and all of a sudden everything went weird."

"Define 'weird'," Julie prompted, as she scooped soy yogurt and protein powder into the blender.

"The whole room went black, and it smelled funny. Like a dungeon. And I heard footsteps." He wiped his hand over his mouth and shook his head. "I must have nodded off or something. Either that or I'm crazy. And I don't have insurance enough to be crazy."

"You're probably low on vitamins," Julie said, her tone scolding. "And you should cut out dairy and gluten for the rest of the week."

"When did dairy and gluten start making people hallucinate?" Miles asked, a little more caustically than he meant to.

"We aren't meant to digest bovine enzymes. You'd be amazed at how your health would improve if you gave them up. And more people have gluten allergies than we think." She turned on the blender, and for a moment the sound was like a cleansing white noise. Then she snapped it off, poured the shake into a glass and brought it over to Miles. "Drink this, and tell me you don't feel better."

It tasted like sweet grass. But Miles drank it anyway, willing to do just about anything right now so long as the smells and light stayed right. When Julie sat down across from him with a tattered paisley bag, though, Miles held up his hands.

"No," Miles said, wiping his soy mustache away. "Julie, I hate those things."

"There's wisdom in Tarot cards." She pulled shiny black cards from the bag and shuffled them. "If you're hallucinating, they can help you figure out what messages your mind is trying to send you."

Miles glowered but said nothing more, tensing as he watched the cards slide through her hands. *They don't work*, he reminded himself. And they didn't. The last time Julie had done this, she'd told him he'd meet his true love in a journey across water and that he'd soon be in the job of his dreams after a period of struggle. Almost immediately after that he'd been laid off, and there was nothing dreamy about working for Patty. He'd taken a journey across water, too, just before the layoff: a gay cruise down in the Keys. He'd come home with nothing but crabs.

But even though he knew it was all garbage, Miles still felt uneasy whenever Julie laid out his cards, and this time was no exception. He held his breath as she laid out first one card, then another, then another, until five cards lay between them, each one more beautiful and terrible than the last.

Julie frowned.

"Are they bad?" Miles asked, trying to sound nonchalant. He couldn't stop looking at them. They certainly *looked* bad. The names weren't helpful, either. "Devil." "The Tower." The next one had no name, just a shitload of swords sticking into someone's back as they lay in a pool of their own blood. The fourth was the only good one: it was called "The Star," and it looked quite beautiful, actually.

But the fifth card was "Death."

Julie caught him looking at the last card and shook her head. "That card doesn't mean you're going to die. It means change."

"Then why the hell doesn't it say 'Change'?" Miles demanded. He couldn't seem to lift his eyes from the skeletal figure with a scythe riding an equally bony horse.

"Because humans experience all change as if it is a death." But she was still frowning. "What I don't understand is why that's your final outcome card. It'd make perfect sense in your past, because of your job. But your past is apparently full of obsession and lust and greed."

"Thanks."

"The Tower makes sense in the present," Julie went on, ignoring him. "Your whole world is coming down around your ears, and you need to rebuild. But the Ten of Swords *there*?" She tapped the stabbed man absently. "You must still be working through some of your frustration at being laid off. Except I'm wondering if it's not more than that." She tapped again, then shifted her attention to the next card. "*This* one is beautiful. Your heart's desire, your true self. Your wishes come true. But why you're wishing for death, I don't know."

"You said it was change," Miles said, a little desperately.

"*Big* change," Julie said. "Losing your job kind of change. Moving across the country change. Radical restructuring. Essentially, what you've already done."

"No offense," Miles said, "but I don't want to live in your spare bedroom and work in the pawn shop forever."

Julie waved an impatient hand at him. "Right now is a transitional time. But this is saying you need to rebuild again." She tapped the stabbed man again. "First, though, you must face the fears you are trying to hide from."

Miles thought of the manky, pitch-black cavern he'd imagined in the bedroom and felt slightly sick. He pushed the protein shake away. "Julie, you aren't helping. What does this have to do with my hallucinations?"

Julie bit her lip and gathered the cards again. She shut her eyes, murmured under her breath as she shuffled, then abruptly laid down two more cards.

Miles sucked in his breath.

The Devil was back again, looking like a satyr on his throne, holding a naked man and woman prisoner with chains he clasped loosely in one hand. But the other card said "The Emperor," and it was the most beautiful card Miles had ever seen.

The Emperor was cold, but he was so handsome he made Miles's teeth ache. He was tall and thin, his face elegant and cool, his eyes dark and almost invisible inside his sockets. Long golden hair streamed out behind him as if in an unseen wind, a lovely contrast to the fawn and cream colors of his costume. He was sheathed in a soft white robe, and he held a silver scepter in his hand. He stared out from the card and straight into Miles's eyes. And even though Julie's pot of dye still sat on the stove, as Miles stared down at the image of the Emperor, he swore he smelled summer again.

"Two men," Julie said quietly. "You'll meet two men. One of them will be your destruction. The other will be your salvation." She laid down one more card. It was a woman, blindfolded, holding crossed swords above her head. "But do not trust your eyes. Trust in truth, and wisdom, and in your heart."

Miles couldn't stop looking at the golden Emperor. "So I'll either be destroyed or saved, depending on what I chose?"

"No," Julie said, a little faintly. "You'll be destroyed. *Then* saved." She bit her lip and gathered up the cards. "I don't know. Let me do some research. This reading just gets weirder the more I look at it."

Miles ached a little when the Emperor disappeared, but then he blinked and sat back, feeling clearer. "Julie, it's okay. I appreciate all this, really—but I think you're reading too much into it. Pardon the pun." He cleared his throat. "It's all just that I'm still upset over losing my job. It makes sense."

But Julie was shaking her head. "It's more than that, Miles. You have some seriously bad energy here. It's kind of scaring me."

And now you're scaring me right back. "Hey—how about I go into town and see about talking to somebody? I can go to the Unitarian minister or something. He won't charge me, and maybe he can hook me up with a community liaison that can get me a discount counseling rate for the uninsured and unemployed. Will that make you feel better?"

Julie went to the counter and picked up her purse. "Actually, what I want is for you to stop by Katie's. I have a few things I need from her. I'll give you a list."

Miles blinked as Julie handed him a list and a twenty. "What—again?"

"Yes." Julie looked at him expectantly.

"You want me to go *now*?" Miles asked. He gestured to the cards. "That's it? You're just going to tell me I need to metaphorically die and rebuild my whole life, more than I already have, and now go get me some dried bat foot?"

Julie gave him a disapproving look. "There's no such thing as dried bat foot. But yes, I want you to run some errands for me." She pulled his coat off the peg by the door and handed it to him. "And don't worry about Patty. I'll tell her I sent you off for something for the soup. Which is, actually, what you're doing. Somebody didn't fix my food processor." She nudged him. "Go on."

"I'll need to get the keys to the car from Patty," Miles pointed out as he rose, but Julie shook her head.

"Walk," she said. "It's only a half a mile, and it's through town, just before the church where you said you were going anyway," she chided him, when he squeaked in protest. "And it isn't as cold as it has been. The exercise will be good for you." She produced hand-knitted mittens, scarf, and hat. "Go on. If you hurry, you'll be back in time for lunch."

"Julie," Miles complained, but she was already shoving him out the door.

"Vegetable soup and vegan dumplings," she said, sing-song. "With garlic bread from sprouted bean flour."

It sounded vaguely gross in concept, but Miles knew that if Julie made it, it would be amazing. Still. "Julie, this is ridiculous. Why the hell do I have to walk to town? Are you trying to get rid of me?"

"Yes." She slammed the door in his face, and the click of the lock followed.

Miles glared at the door for several seconds, then sighed.

He put on his scarf and his gloves, but he tucked the hat into his pocket. It wasn't that cold, he assured himself, though he did pull the scarf up higher to shield his ears. He grumbled all the way through the trailer park, cursing Julie and her voodoo.

Devils, Emperors, and Towers. And Death that wasn't death. He should never have let her read his cards. It was all stupid. He was just overtired. That was *all*. Anything else was weirder than Julie's tofu brownies. He supposed he should be glad he was getting out of working for the morning. It *was* nice out, if a bit chilly and gloomy. But it was a crisp fall day, and he hadn't been to anything remotely resembling a gym in months. It would do him good to walk. He'd get whatever weird stuff Katie had for him, put up with her making freaky at him and acting like he was possessed, stop by the church and make an appointment, and head home. Easy as that. Then he'd eat lunch, call some of the local dealers he'd bookmarked for the flute, then go work in the pawnshop some more. No more moping.

Leaves and sticks crunched beneath his feet, and Miles smiled. This was his life now, and he'd live it. Devil and Emperor free. He looked up, smug and satisfied with his declaration.

The trailer park was gone. He was in the middle of the forest.

It smelled of summer.

Miles stumbled backward. What the *fuck*? The path leading back to the park had disappeared, somehow becoming nothing but trees. How? He'd been on the road! He wasn't anywhere *near* the woods. Yeah, he'd been lost in thought, but not this lost.

In the distance he heard the echo of cloven feet clicking as they moved against stone.

He heard an animal snort. Hot breath brushed against his neck, and Miles smelled no more summer, just the dirty, matted stink of wet animal hair and rot.

The Emperor. And the Devil.

One will destroy you. One will save you.

"Help!" Miles pushed off the tree and stumbled forward. "Help—someone, anyone! Please—" He heard the snort again and yelped, then fumbled in his pockets. Somehow, it didn't surprise him to find the flute box there.

Miles didn't stop to think; he opened the box and brought the silver instrument to his cold, trembling lips. Part of his brain insisted this was a really stupid thing to do, to stop and play a flute when something scary chased him, but the move was almost a compulsion. He couldn't *not* play the flute right now.

Please, he thought, swallowing fear as he shuddered a breath into the mouthpiece. It made a thin, mournful wail in answer.

He heard the footsteps coming closer. He could smell it now, so clearly, and when he closed his eyes, he knew somehow he was back in that dark dungeon, that the monster was there with him, and it was coming for him.

Please, help me, he pleaded, and blew a clear, high note on the flute.

The beast snorted in rage and reached for him.

Miles blew again, trilling desperately, then braced for impact. When a shadow fell across his face, he winced, but when no blow fell, he opened his eyes.

The smell was gone. The forest was still there, but the menacing presence had vanished. In front of him stood a shining white and silver sleigh, lined with white flowers and silver bells, silver ribbons leading to two beautiful gray horses.

In the center of the sleigh sat a man. He was the spitting image of the Emperor from Julie's cards, except this man was dressed in silver, not white. But other than that he was the same. Same long white hair, same hauteur, same elegance and beauty and command.

"I'm dreaming." Miles lifted his hands and stared at them, at the flute glinting in the sunlight that filtered through the trees. "I have to be dreaming."

The Emperor laughed, an elegant, crisp sound that snuck under Miles's skin and made his blood purr. "Then let me be the first to compliment you on your charming and articulate subconscious." He smiled at Miles and patted the seat beside him. "Come, Miles Larson, and ride with me."

Miles took a step back. "How do you know my name?"

The man looked amused. "Wouldn't your subconscious know everything about you?" When Miles just stared at him, the man clucked his tongue and nodded curtly. "Come. Don't waste time. Get in, Miles, or I won't be responsible for what happens to you."

There was something funny about the way he phrased that, and Miles wanted to question it, but the underlying urgency to the man's voice made him pause. "Is—is he coming back? The other one?"

The Emperor's eyes went very dark, and they glimmered. For a moment they seemed to have no iris at all: they were just silver-black portals into his skull. "This is my last request," he said, in a voice that echoed across the forest.

Miles felt the light darken, and in the distance, he heard the *click, click* of hooves again. Terror seized him, and he looked down to the flute, thinking maybe if he blew it again, that would help.

The flute was gone.

Behind him the beast huffed, then roared, and with a cry of his own, Miles ran forward to the sleigh and into the Emperor's waiting arms.

THE EMPEROR CAUGHT Miles with a graceful strength which, combined with the summer-fresh scent of him, made Miles shudder, but not with fear. It had been a long, long time since a man had held him in his arms, and the fact that the Emperor was pretty much extracted from his libido's idea of a perfect man only heightened Miles's awareness and filled him with a primal sort of need. His hands, which were caught between their chests, turned so his fingers could dig into the soft material of the Emperor's vest.

"I am flattered," the man said in a patient, amused voice, "but I am not, I must tell you, an emperor."

Miles drew back and looked up at the man in surprise. "How—I didn't say anything—!"

The man looked amused. "But this can't be happening, as you say. If I'm not real, then it's nothing, is it, to peek inside your mind. I can hear everything you're thinking, Miles. Everything." His smile darkened, and he ran a finger down Miles's cheek, sliding it over to catch the edge of his bottom lip. "Though I admit I like the idea of being your emperor. If I were, I could make you do whatever I wanted."

The finger at Miles's lip tugged insistently at the flesh, and Miles parted his lips. *This can't be happening*, he thought again, and the man smiled, reading the thought.

"Yes. It's just a dream. Give yourself to the dream, Miles."

Miles wanted to. If this was a dream, it was the most vivid, wonderful dream he'd ever had. Whoever this man was, he was gorgeous. He was charming, too, which Miles had never been able to resist. This man wanted Miles. He was handsome, clean, wicked, and tugging at Miles's bottom lip. Oh, God, but Miles wanted to lie down right there and present his body as an offering.

The man's eyes darkened. "How readily we progress." His finger fell away from Miles's mouth, but then the man's whole hand rested over the center of

Miles's chest. He gazed upon Miles with a thoughtful expression. "Would you truly offer yourself to me so quickly?"

It's just a dream, Miles told himself. But something in the man's face made him pause. What *was* going on here, anyway? What was all this? Who was this guy, subconscious or no? How had Miles ended up in the forest when he'd been heading toward town?

As if his hesitation were a doorway, Miles felt the air shift around him, and in the distance he heard the clicking hooves begin again. He tensed, and to his surprise, so did his companion.

Except his companion was angry, not afraid. He glared, his upper lip curling into a sneer. "Oh, no you don't," he said, his voice soft and dangerous. Then he drew Miles up against his side. "Come, Miles. It's time we were away."

"Away where?" Miles followed the man's gaze off into the forest, but he didn't see anything. Yet he could feel the beast coming toward them, and he pressed harder up against the man's side.

"So many questions." The man leaned forward slightly to catch the silver ribbons that served as reins. He clicked his tongue, and after the horses tossed their heads, they began to walk forward, dragging the sleigh behind them.

Miles frowned down at the ground. "This is never going to work. There isn't any snow—"

He cut himself off as the horses began to move

faster, and as if it were the sort of thing that happened every day, the sleigh lifted effortlessly off the ground.

They were traveling, Miles realized with a strangely sick feeling in his stomach, several inches above the undergrowth of the forest. The horses still advanced with some acknowledgment to gravity, but even that, he realized, was subject to some question. Their hooves hit the ground, but when the ground dipped too low or became too rocky, they rode on the same invisible highway as the sleigh. It was impossible. It couldn't happen. But it was.

"Poor Miles." The man stroked Miles's hair. "Just lie back and let me take care of you. Soon we'll be somewhere very pleasant, and all of this will just be a bad memory."

The horses were moving even faster now, so fast that Miles thought he was going to be sick. But when he settled into the man's shoulder, his stomach calmed down.

"You may call me Terris," the man said gently, but even at his gentlest, there was no erasing the wickedness beneath his silky undertone.

Terris. The name was familiar, and Miles's brain raced to remember why. Then he recalled the website and the darkness that had come when he clicked on it. Miles drew back to the edge of the sleigh, cold with terror.

As soon as he was away from the warm shelter of Terris's arms, he felt the hot breath of the beast against his neck, felt the dank cold of the marble dungeon closing around him—

He cried out as Terris yanked him back against his body, and this time Miles didn't fight him. "What's happening? I don't understand—if this is a dream, I want to wake up."

"You're straddling two worlds." Terris's voice was curt and clipped. "You've drawn him in as well as me, but I warn you, Miles, he who chases you and I cannot live together." He looked behind the sleigh, and he murmured bitterly beneath his breath in a language Miles didn't know. "You must banish him, darling. Send him away, so we may be in peace."

Miles lifted his head from Terris's shoulder and looked behind the sleigh. He cried out in terror.

The Devil was chasing them. It was a great horned beast, full of hair and hooves, and it ran straight for Miles, keeping up with the sleigh and gaining. It was naked, and between its legs hung a cock as big as a child's arm, framed by huge, hairy ball sacs. But it had a human's face, visible even as it was shrouded by over-grown beard and eyebrows. The body was the most menacing thing Miles had ever seen.

The face was heartbreaking. Miles was moved despite himself.

"Send him away," Terris said, his voice a gentle command. His hand slid up Miles's thigh. "Send him away, or he'll catch us, and then I will have to go. And if I leave, someone much worse than either of us will come for you."

"There's another monster?"

"This place is full of strange creatures, but there are only three of us interested in you right now. Only one of us can have you. Whom do you wish to claim you, Miles?"

Miles watched the hooves of the beast hammer into the ground, watched that heavy cock sway like a weapon, and he shrank a little closer to Terris. He couldn't even let himself think about this third person. But it wasn't just terror staying him—the face of the beast chasing the sleigh kept drawing him back.

"What happened to him?" Miles asked.

"He chose to get out of the sleigh."

Miles curled his fingers around the intricate silver grillwork on the top of the sleigh seat, letting the metal cut into his skin as he stared back in a strange mixture of terror and pity. That wasn't the whole story, that much was clear. But it was also clear Terris wasn't going to explain anything further.

"That's because there isn't time. At this moment, Miles, it comes down to this: do you want to be with me, or with him? Or with the one who made the beast?"

Miles bit his lip. He realized, to his shock, that the answer was that part of him *did* want to go with the beast. Something about the hideous creature—who was now less than twenty feet behind them—tugged at Miles's heart.

"He'll consume you, if he catches you," Terris said matter-of-factly. "Whatever pity you feel for him won't do you any good once he has you beneath him."

The beast reached out with hands full of claws. Its mouth foamed, and as the beast drew closer, the sorrow in its eyes gave way to desperation and a ferocity that quickly doused Miles's sympathy.

He tightened his hands against the grillwork and shook his head. "Go. Go—please!"

Terris rolled his eyes. "Oh, yes. That will work."

"What *will* work?" Miles cried, starting to panic now. The beast was so close that it could leap onto the sleigh, if it wanted. Miles could smell the stink of it, sharper and ranker than ever.

"Banish him. Tell him you don't want him."

"I don't want you!" Miles cried, with feeling. But even with the sight of that drooling mouth, those claws, and that horrible cock, Miles couldn't quite forget those eyes. The edge of empathy remained in his voice, and the beast stayed.

Terris sighed and turned to Miles. "You'll have to show him, then. Show him you don't want him. Show him that you want someone else."

"*Nā!*"

The cry came from the beast, and it tore at Miles: the voice was rough and wild, but it was undeniably human. This beast was once a man.

The beast leapt, landing on the back of the sleigh, now just a little more than an arm's reach from Miles.

Miles cried out and moved as far forward in the sleigh as he could. He tangled in the horses' ribbons, knocking the sleigh from side to side as their course became erratic. Miles pitched against the rail, and at the back of the sleigh, the beast struggled to keep from falling off. Only Terris remained unaffected, moving with the motion of the raucous sleigh as if it were the easiest thing in the world.

"Time to choose," Terris said, calm as ever.

"*Nese!*" the beast roared again. Still fighting to stay on the sleigh, he dared to extend one arm toward Miles. His eyes were small and sad, and wild. "*Nese, gástlufu! Nese!*"

Miles ached at the yearning in the beast's voice, and without thinking, he began to reach.

The beast was huffing now, its hairy nostrils flaring. "*Gástlufu!*" it said gruffly. "*Gástlufu!*" But there was a funny edge to whatever it was the beast was saying.

Terris snorted a derisive laugh.

Miles held his breath, watching the beast's face. But it only huffed and whined, pawing at the back of the seat now as it tried to get to Miles. "*Gástlufu!*" it said gruffly. It looked at Miles, and all the sorrow was gone, replaced with thick, black lust. "*Gástlufu! Gástlufu! Gástlufu!*" It said the word over and over, and Miles watched in horror as it thrust its hips against the side of the sleigh, its grotesque cock expanding with every plunge.

Miles turned quickly to Terris. "And you? What will

you do to me?"

Terris smiled, a slow and sultry gesture that, despite the terror of the beast, made Miles feel hot and liquid inside.

"I will do whatever you like." He leaned forward. "*Whatever* you like, darling."

Miles reached for Terris. "You," he said, his voice only wavering a little. "I want you."

The beast cried out in rage and reached for Miles again.

"You!" he shouted, and caught Terris's hand. "I want you, Terris. I want you. Not him."

The beast made a strange mewling sound, and Miles knew if he looked at it, he would see the sorrow, and he would be lost.

Pushing aside the guilt the sound had aroused, he shut his eyes.

The sleigh jerked, but this time Miles moved with it as easily as Terris. He heard an anguished cry, and then the sleigh shot forward. He opened his eyes in time to see the beast rolling away into the woods. He yelped in pain and screamed in misery, and the sound went like a lightning strike into Miles's soul.

Terris caught Miles's face and turned it toward his own. "You've chosen me," he said, patiently. "Now tell me what you want."

"What is this?" Miles whispered. "Who is he? Who are you? What's happening to me?"

"He is the bad dream. I am the good dream."

Miles could still hear the beast's cries in the distance, but he could feel Terris's hands moving against his skin, across his cheek, down to his neck, and against the fabric of his jeans, moving up his thigh. He had lost his gloves and scarf somehow, and his coat was open, making it easy for Terris to slide his hand beneath Miles's shirt and explore the tender flesh of his stomach. Behind them Miles heard the thrashing of the monster in the underbrush, but he also heard the soft jingling of the horses' harness and the even softer sound of his own breath coming faster and faster as Terris touched him. *I want to kiss him*, he thought, the urge primal and deep, born of a lust for the beauty that was the man before him. *I want to kiss Terris. I want Terris to kiss me.*

A soft, wicked smile played against Terris's lips. "With pleasure." He leaned forward to press those lips against Miles's own.

In the distance the beast cried out again, but he was very far away now, and Terris was so close, and so warm. *And wet.* Miles opened his mouth at the urging of Terris's silky tongue, sighing as he let the other man inside. Terris smelled of the spice of summer, like rain, like sweet and wonderful release. Miles sighed and opened wider to him, and when Terris slid his hand between Miles's thighs, he opened for him there too.

"That's the way." Terris trailed kisses down the curve of Miles's throat, reached inside Miles's underwear to take him firmly in hand. "Let go to me, Miles.

Forget everything else and ride away with me in a beautiful, sensual dream."

Miles did. He shut his ears to the beast's cries, which had grown plaintive again, and he surrendered to the magic of Terris's mouth and hands as the horses pushed off the ground and into the sky, their silver ribbon reins flapping uselessly in the air beside them.

MILES DIDN'T KNOW how long he'd been kissing Terris, but when he finally came up for air and dared a look around, he saw that the sleigh was skimming across a silver lake and heading toward a white, gleaming castle settled on a distant emerald shore. It was startlingly beautiful, so much so that it momentarily distracted him from Terris, which was a serious statement in and of itself. When he realized that he'd stopped the kiss, he turned back guiltily, but Terris didn't seem to mind, and regarded it with satisfaction.

"Do you like it?" Terris's fingers were still twining in Miles's hair, but idly now. His other hand still moved up and down Miles's exposed cock, a tender rather than an erotic touch. His delicate fingers skimmed over Miles's balls and teased them with an expert's mastery. "Do you like the dream I've made for you, Miles?"

"You did this?" Miles sucked in a breath as Terris's finger slid behind his balls. "You—you made this?"

"Oh yes. But this is nothing, darling. So much more waits for you." His finger slid farther back, teasing but not touching Miles's entrance.

Miles gripped the seat and tried to keep his eyes from rolling back inside his head. "What—" He jerked as Terris came close again, but he didn't move away. "What is this? You said I'm dreaming? But how? I left the house, I was awake—"

"There are many ways to dream, Miles," he said, his voice chiding. But then he sighed and withdrew his hand. "It wouldn't be helpful for you to be too upset, so we'll slow things down a bit, shall we?" He patted Miles's thigh. "Do yourself up, and we'll go explore the castle. All this will keep for later."

Miles shifted on the seat as he did up his jeans, feeling foolish but not knowing quite why. He kept reaching for reason and logic, but the more he tried, the more lost he became. And all it did, in the end, was drag his attention back to the beast.

"Don't think about him." Terris lounged in his seat, the silver ribbon-reins held casually in his right hand. "When you think of him, it draws him back."

"Who is he? Why was he after me? Why are you here? Why am *I* here? Where *is* here?"

"Philosophy!" Terris lolled his head to his shoulder and gave Miles a weary look. "Darling, it's a dream. How many of your dreams are logical?"

"It feels more real than any dream I've ever had."

"Even as real as the one you had in Atlanta?" Terris asked, as he reached down between them and picked up a small box from the floor.

"Which dream in Atlanta? I lived there ten years." Miles watched as Terris put the box into his own lap. The box was made of silver and tied with a glittering white ribbon. It made Miles think of *The Lion, the Witch, and the Wardrobe*, and as soon as he put that together with the sleigh and the castle, he realized that Terris really did make a pretty good White Witch.

Terris laughed. "Except Edward didn't get a hand job, did he?" He held the box out to Miles. "Here, darling. This is for you."

Miles took the box carefully, trying to be wary, but he couldn't help feeling eager. It was a beautiful present, the most elegant and classy kind of present that he'd always wanted but had never received. Which was a stupid thing to think.

"Why is it stupid to want something nice?" Terris nudged his hand toward the ribbon. "Go on. Open it, and enjoy yourself."

Miles put his fingers to the ribbon, but he didn't pull. He looked up at Terris instead. "What did you mean, the dream in Atlanta? Which dream?"

"Your whole life was a dream while you were there. Just as it is now." When Miles sputtered, Terris laughed again and touched his cheek. "You're so charming when you're obstinate. Go on then, darling. Tell me about some other dream from that time that I could mean."

Miles tried, not sure what he was looking for but determined to somehow prove Terris wrong, because that was absolutely ridiculous, to imply he'd *dreamed* that he'd worked in Atlanta. He tried to think of one dream, even a boring one, to offer up, but honestly, he couldn't come up with anything. Nothing he remembered, anyway. It was odd to think he hadn't dreamed in ten years, but apparently he hadn't.

But he *had* lived there. He *had!* He'd paid rent, for crying out loud! Besides, if he were going to dream he lived somewhere, it wouldn't be in *Atlanta.*

"You don't need to be asleep to dream." Terris kissed Miles's cheek. "Don't worry yourself about that. There's nothing to be gained. Open your present so I can see you smile."

Miles looked down at the beautiful silver box. He almost hated to take it apart. "What's in it?"

"If you open it, you'll find out," Terris suggested.

But what could it be? What in the world would Terris give him, and why? Jewelry? Candy? Magic dust? Sex toys?

Terris, as always reading Miles's thoughts, chuckled. It was a very sexy sound.

Miles tugged at the ribbon. But as the silver glinted in the light of a pale sun Miles had yet to see, the strange silver flute so tangled in all this flashed briefly in his mind.

Terris's hand slammed over the top of Miles's own, and when Miles looked up at him, the other man's face was hard and cold.

"*Never,*" he said, his voice an angry whisper, "never

so much as think of that again."

The frigid fury in Terris's countenance was so great that Miles didn't even think to question why. Nodding, he felt great relief when Terris's hand—now ice cold—retreated.

"I'm sorry," Miles said, more from fear than anything else.

Terris waved his hand in dismissal, and he smiled again as he nodded to the silver box. "Now, no more stalling. Open your present, or I'll take it away."

Tugging the ribbon, Miles released it from the bow. Heart pounding in anticipation, he flicked the catch on the edge of the box and opened the lid.

A long, thin, glittering chain lay inside.

It was brilliantly beautiful, glinting on its purple velvet pillow, and when Miles lifted it gingerly by his fingers, it felt as if he lifted a feather. The chain was so thin he could hardly see the links, and it seemed impossible that it could be strong enough to hold up the gleaming silver-and-pearl ring that dangled from the link in the center, but it was, and it did.

Miles shook his head, almost unable to speak. "It's beautiful."

"It's yours." Terris took it carefully from Miles's hands and lifted it. "Lean forward, darling, and I'll drape it around you."

"There's no clasp," Miles said, but bent forward anyway, eager to have the chain around his neck.

"It doesn't need one," Terris said, as he wrapped

the chain around Miles's throat. It wasn't tight, but it was snug, and when Terris lifted his hands and sat back, Miles reached up and felt the necklace. It was so thin it felt like one chain, even when looped around the four or five times Terris had wound it. He felt the ring sitting there, and when he touched it, he felt all his worries easing out of him, his mind settling into a blissful state of calm.

Terris smiled at him and stroked his hair. "As beautiful as you are." He lifted the silver box. "The lid has a mirror—go on, see how lovely it looks against your skin."

Miles looked at himself, touching the ring and chain some more as he did so. It did make him look lovely. Like a fairy prince. It was the sort of look he'd wanted for himself when he was ten, the look that everyone had shamed out of him. Looking at himself now, adult, grown, sitting in a magic sleigh next to the most handsome man he'd ever seen, whom he'd been kissing and letting touch him like a lover—Miles swallowed hard and shook his head.

"I don't care that this is a dream," he whispered. "I don't want this to end. Ever."

Terris smiled and shut the box. "Then it won't."

Miles knew this couldn't be right. Nothing in life came this easy, not even in a dream, and even dreams couldn't last. He tried to think of what cues he had missed, of what stupid mistake he had made and let himself be caught in a trap, but his mind refused to land on anything, too caught up in the way the sun danced off Terris's hair, in the delicious weight of the necklace against his neck, in the memory of how Terris's mouth had felt against his own and his hand on Miles's body.

Terris smiled his wicked smile. "Dear Miles. It need not only be a memory." He drew Miles forward with a finger curled beneath his chin.

It can't be this easy, but it is for now. Miles shut his eyes as he gave himself once more to Terris.

CHAPTER FOUR

It does not matter how we go,
only that you love me so.
By shining sea, by falling star—
take me lover, where you are.

T HE SLEIGH, AFTER gliding effortlessly across the lake, pulled itself up to the doors of the castle, which opened of their own accord as Miles and Terris approached, allowing the horses to draw them inside and land gracefully in a white marble foyer full of light.

The light came from the hundreds of windows lining the spire above them, and from the walls flanking the split staircase curving around and landing on either side of the blood-red carpet where the sleigh had stopped. The windows up high were clear, but the ones on the stairs were stained glass, and they depicted, to Miles's surprise, several discreet and yet highly suggestive poses by lovers. What surprised Miles was that all the couples were male.

"Is this some sort of gay fairyland?" Miles asked as

Terris helped him out of the sleigh. "Or is this more stuff I'm dreaming? Because if this is in my head, I clearly don't realize my own creative potential."

"The forest is yours. The lake and this castle are not." Terris took Miles's arm and led him toward a pair of crystal-laden doors beneath the stairs. "Allow me to give you a tour." When Miles glanced back at the horses, Terris gently turned him away again. "Never mind the sleigh. It will be taken care of."

So there were servants here after all. Except Miles had never been inside a place that felt emptier. He felt a twinge of uncertainty, but then he reached up and touched the ring on the chain of his necklace, and he eased again, especially when the crystal doors opened and Miles stepped into the wonderland that hid behind them.

The room had high ceilings like the foyer, but this room was huge, and it was full of flowers. There were plants everywhere, most of them hanging in baskets set in tiers, forming columns that lined the gleaming black-and-white checkered floor. The flowers that bloomed from the baskets were lush, most of them boasting huge blooms that hung like trumpets or exploded in fat bunches. The flowers were of countless colors, but most of them were white, accented sometimes by pale blue flowers that looked like ice. Delicate white benches lined the sides of the room, and several velvet-lined ones were grouped around a stunning fountain in the center whose jets alternated in sequences of spray, backlit by some source Miles could not see.

"This is the main audience room." Terris gestured across the vast space.

"So there *are* other people here?" Miles asked.

"Not just now." Terris reached up to a nearby basket and plucked a pale orange trumpet, then held it up to Miles's ear.

Miles brushed it away. "No thank you."

Terris clucked his tongue. "But it would so become you." He shrugged, then tucked it behind his own ear and took Miles's arm again. "Let me show you the rest of the palace."

"Whose palace is it?" Miles asked.

"It belongs to the Lord of Dreams," Terris said matter-of-factly. "It was he who called you here, he whom you accepted."

"Accepted?" Miles echoed, not liking the sound of this.

"Yes." Terris reached out for another flower, this one small and brilliant blue. He held it tauntingly before Miles's face. "What about this one?"

Why did Terris want him to wear a flower? Miles shook his head. "Who is the Lord of Dreams? What do you mean, I accepted him?"

"The Lord of Dreams is the owner of this castle. And you accepted him."

"But—" Miles faltered, getting lost in this conversation. "But—I didn't—"

Terris sighed, then tucked the flower into one of

the loops of Miles's jeans. The motion made his fingers brush against Miles tantalizingly, and Miles stopped trying to speak and held still, enjoying the touch.

"You're very sensual, aren't you?" Terris's fingers brushed Miles's stomach as he ran his index finger up the center of Miles's chest. "You enjoy being touched as much as you enjoy sex itself."

Miles shrugged and looked away, letting his gaze fall on an urn full of violets. "Sure."

Terris laughed. "And shy. You shouldn't be, not here, and not with me."

Miles shifted uncomfortably. "I just—this is all a little weird."

Terris laughed again. Annoyed, Miles went to the violets and stroked their petals.

"So is this Lord of Dreams here?" Miles glanced back at Terris as a thought occurred to him. "Are *you*—?"

All Terris's amusement fled. "Absolutely not." He glanced around, looking almost nervous for the first time. "I would never presume to claim His Lordship's title."

Miles wanted to ask what this Lord was like—Was he fey, or was he some immortal being like Neil Gaiman's Sandman?—but Terris's uneasy expression kept him silent. When Terris recovered himself, he took Miles's arm again.

"Perhaps you would like to see one of the more private salons?"

"Sure," Miles said.

As they passed a bed of white roses, Terris plucked one, discarded the thorns, and held it up once more to Miles's ear.

"You won't rest until I wear one, will you?" Miles asked.

In answer, Terris leaned forward and pressed an almost chaste kiss to Miles's lips. Miles shut his eyes, drinking in the fresh summer scent of his companion, the aroma mingling now with the soft perfume of the orange trumpet hanging behind his head. When Terris drew back, Miles felt the petals of the white rose brushing against his cheek.

Miles felt, for one moment, a sense of unease. It was as if a part of him had been crouching in the back of his own mind, watching everything that was happening, and after some consideration, it registered a verdict: Something very fishy was going on.

Things like this don't happen, his thoughts insisted. *Not even in dreams. Not like this. Anything this good has a razor in it. Only a fool would think anything different.*

Terris's eyes sparkled, but in a rather unpleasant way. "I thought as much." He brushed his fingers against the rose. "Is that the sum of your objection? Anything else in there, any other warnings aching to be heard?"

"I—I don't—" Miles took a step backward, glancing around nervously at the flower-laden hall. Suddenly it seemed *too* lush, the perfume of so many flowers not exotic but thick and cloying. "It just doesn't make sense. It can't be good. There has to be something you aren't telling me."

Terris nodded. "Would you like me to tell you now?" He crooked his finger. "Come closer."

Miles did.

Terris's eyes went completely black, and he plucked the rose from Miles's ear.

Miles gasped, clutching at his ear in pain. He expected to feel blood and a great gash, but there was nothing. And yet as he watched Terris twirl the flower between his fingers, he realized that something was gone, something was not in his head which had been there seconds before.

Memories. Thoughts. He put them in the flower.

Terris's black eye winked. Then he dropped the rose onto the ground and crushed it ruthlessly beneath the heel of an elegant silver shoe. "And now they're all gone," he said.

Miles blinked. His head didn't hurt anymore, but he felt a little lightheaded. He looked up at Terris in confusion. "What just happened?"

Terris smiled. "I asked if you would like me to take you into one of the salons and make love to you. But if you'd rather not, I won't be offended."

Heat rushed through Miles. "No—please, I *do* want that."

Terris's smile darkened, and he extended his hand. "Then please, allow me to lead the way."

Miles took his hand, feeling dizzy still, but eager and happy too. It was a funny sort of happiness, though, like bubble gum. Light and silly, ready to pop at any moment. But Terris was stroking his arm and whispering where he'd like to kiss him first, and he told himself he shouldn't care.

He paused at the doorway and looked back, not sure what he searched for. When he looked down and saw a ruined white rose lying there, for a moment he felt sad. But then Terris touched his hand, and he didn't care anymore.

As the crystal doors shut, he had a sudden flash of vision—he saw the rose again, and he saw a hairy clawed hand reaching out from beneath a veil of foliage, grabbing it and stealing the ruined petals away. But when Miles blinked, the vision was gone, as was his memory of it, and he didn't think of it again as he followed Terris down another bright white hall.

MILES HAD A brief view of a room full of windows and sun and silver velvet drapes, and then Terris pressed Miles back onto a padded bench, trailing open-mouthed kisses down his jaw. Miles shut his eyes and surrendered.

Terris was everything that had ever gotten Miles in trouble with a man. The cool hauteur, the silky, wicked demeanor, even the slippery wit: every man Miles had ever wanted had been this way. They were arrogant.

They were slightly twisted. They liked to play their lovers like violins and discard them like overused rosin. They were handsome and sleek and styled. But at the same time, Terris was unlike any man Miles had ever been with. The difference between them and Terris was twofold: none of them had been quite *so* all those things together, and not a one of them had wooed Miles like this.

The presents, the flowers, the casual flattery, the lazy lure into letting go—it was as if Terris had a list of all the things Miles had longed for and never received and was giving them to him one by one. He had done everything but ply him with expensive champagne and chocolate on the beach beneath a starry sky. Miles hardly cared, though, because now Terris was making love to him; and just as he had met all Miles's romantic fantasies, so was he doing in sex.

Miles had known many, many men, and he'd slept with even more. Sometimes he felt like he was some sort of desperate fisherman, constantly casting out, trying to find that one man who could ease the ache inside him. It was ridiculously romantic and undoubtedly full of unexplored psychoses, which was why he tried not to think of it.

Terris was unearthing those old yearnings, too, and meeting every one. He held Miles down, hard enough to thrill him but not enough to hurt him. He licked and sucked at every sensitive, aching spot, lingering on the long muscle that went taut when he arched his neck, on the divot beneath Miles's clavicle. He slid his fingers down the planes of Miles's chest so softly that they felt like satin against his skin, skimmed them back again and brushed teasing, tender circles around Miles's nipples.

"You are so lovely, Miles," Terris whispered as he drew Miles up to peel his shirt away, then pressed him back to the bench again. His voice was sultry and soft, his lips brushing against Miles's tender throat. "Lovely to look at, lovely to hold. Give yourself to me, Miles. Lie back and let me love you."

Miles had no arguments with this. He was already lying back as much as was physically possible—as a sort of compromise, he arched his back, bringing his body closer to Terris's erotic exploration. He gasped when he felt Terris's tongue slide down his sternum, and he trembled when the trajectory angled off toward his hard and aching nipple. But Terris, still plumbing the depths of Miles secret desires, did not hit his target right away. Rather, he teased his way home, nipping, licking, whispering incoherent endearments against Miles's skin, brushing near the eager bud but never reaching it. He waited until Miles was crying out, alternating between tortured moans and whispered pleas, and then, only then, did he close his lips over the tiny peak.

Once Terris claimed his prize, however, he was relentless. He swirled his tongue around, then over the bud; he suckled hard, then released, then suckled again.

He drew the peak between his teeth and found the white-hot line between pain and bone-melting pleasure. And all the while, his fingers teased its companion, tugging, kneading, pinching in tandem to the torture of the one within his mouth. He brought Miles to the very edge of his endurance, until he was little more than a pulsing shaft of need—and then he lifted his head, adjusted his angle, and brought his mouth back down to give the same treatment to the other breast.

When Terris finally let his mouth slide down the rest of the way to Miles's waist, Miles was so lost he barely knew his own name, and he knew no more fear. He eagerly helped Terris shed his clothing—Miles's only, which was, of course, another secret fantasy. When Terris knelt, fully dressed, between Miles's parted thighs, Miles lifted his head and watched, aching with pleasure as Terris slid his long, slender fingers over Miles's red, aching cock. He shuddered as Terris traced the veins, the bulbous head, the cleft at the underside of the glans—Miles surrendered in a cascading cry of ecstasy as Terris ran his tongue along the length, circled the rim of the head, then took the whole organ through his lips, into his mouth, into his throat.

It was the fellatio of fellatios. Just the right pressure, just the right hint of teeth without them actually being there. Tongue everywhere it should be, hands braced *just right* against his thighs, pressing them back and wide, opening his hole but not touching him there, hinting at what was yet to come. But even that was just a tease—this was all about cock: cock suckled, cock teased, cock worshiped, taken deep into Terris's beautiful, beautiful mouth, his lips spread wide around it, sliding, glistening with spit and slightly swollen from their work. Every so often Miles would lift his head to take in the sight, and the perfection of it would shatter him all over again, and he would collapse back to the bench, waves of pleasure crashing over him with such regularity now he could have been a sea.

But just as Miles was about to climb another crest, Terris stopped and lifted his head.

"Darling," he said, his voice teasing, crooning, and breathless, "darling, why are you still holding back? Am I doing something wrong?"

Miles gave a weak, strangled laugh. "God no. Nothing has ever been more right."

"Then why—?"

Why aren't you coming? That was what Terris wanted to know, but Miles didn't have an answer. He shook his head, weakly. "I don't know. By rights I should have blown into pieces by now." He slid a heavy hand down his abdomen and caught Terris's hand with half-numb fingers. "It's not you. I'm sorry—don't be hurt."

"I'm not hurt," Terris said, his tone oddly careful. "I only wish to please you, Miles. It's very important to me."

Miles opened his eyes and looked blearily up at his lover. "There is no questioning that. Terris—" His throat became thick with emotion too intense to express, and he shook his head. "Please. I don't know how someone like me ever attracted someone like you, even in a dream—I could never be disappointed in you. Everything about you pleases me. *Everything.*"

Terris was not moved by this speech; if anything, his countenance became more shuttered. But before Miles could wonder at this, Terris rose and smiled. "Then let me please you more." He began to undo the ties to his shirt.

Miles propped himself on his elbows and watched, his breathing narrowing to shallow, desperate gasps as Terris removed his clothing and revealed his body. Everything about Terris was so right it almost hurt. His skin, so smooth, so rich and yet so pale. His lips, still swollen, parted just enough to entice without being too much. His shoulders, broad and yet slender. His chest, beautiful, sculpted, like a marble David, not the jarring bulges that looked too much like an actual washboard. His absolutely hairless chest, sloped and perfect, drawing the gaze down to his navel—on a stomach perfectly, achingly flat—and then his groin, where soft blond hair teased in a small tuft of curls before—

The panel of Terris's crisp white trousers fell away, and Miles groaned.

Oh, God.

Terris's cock: uncut, straight, rising slowly as his arousal grew. Pale, but now flush as it lifted, the foreskin pulling back just slightly as the organ it surrounded swelled. The ball sac: bare, raw, perfectly shaped, just resting, so soft and sweet and the size of Miles's mouth, which ached to know them.

Perfect.

The trousers fell to the floor, revealing Terris's thighs, and his knees, and then Terris moved forward, his naked body sliding over Miles's own.

Flesh on flesh—the heat of Miles's skin against the cool, sleek slide of Terris, as thighs, chests, and, of course, cocks met. Miles, overcome, reached up, helpless, and Terris caught his hands at the same time he caught his mouth, diving inside, seeking, claiming, and through it all, begging.

Surrender to me. Surrender to me, Miles. Surrender to me.

Miles did: over, and over, and over, but it never seemed to be enough. He moved when Terris wanted him to, where he wanted him to—at some point the bench became a bed, wide and thick and cased in silk, and Miles didn't even question it, just gave himself to the dream that was Terris, that was sex with Terris. He was lost, so lost, and he never wanted to be found. But it was not enough.

Terris lifted from the kiss and stared down at him, studying his face. At Miles's neck, his fingers toyed with the necklace and ring he had placed there. Then he smiled and kissed Miles's nose.

"But of course. I don't know why I didn't think of it before." He let go of the ring and reached down to lightly slap Miles's rump. "On your side, darling."

Miles rolled toward Terris, unsure of what was

happening, but willing—very, very willing. Terris shift-ed himself alongside, their bodies reversed so that he had his mouth at Miles's cock again, but lying so that this time his own was available to Miles as well. Miles needed no encouragement or instruction. He took the beautiful rod in his hand, cradled the balls, and took his shaft deep into his mouth. When Terris did the same, he thought, *here, here is where I will surrender, where I will give myself to him.*

But he didn't.

Oh, he gasped, and he cried out, and he became slick as a seal with his own sweat, but he did not come. He made passionate love to Terris's cock, teasing it, sucking it, palming it, pulling back the foreskin with his tongue. He toyed with Terris's slit, and he sucked as if he could pull the spunk out of him, all the while thrust-ing and shuddering at Terris's equally intense onslaught. Miles was so aroused he was lost in pleas-ure-pain. He had stopped being dazzled by the perfection of it all and had given over to the experience itself, but even then he did not come. And he didn't even mind. But it was driving Terris crazy.

He broke away and climbed back around to Miles's mouth, his kisses desperate now. "Darling," he gasped, taking their cocks together in his hand, guiding their joined thrusts. "Darling—what is it you desire? What is it that you need, which I lack?"

But Miles couldn't answer. He only pushed his hips in time to Terris's urging and rode on, sure that he could do this forever. Even when Terris gripped his chin and looked down at him in alarm, he only grinned and kept on thrusting. Forever, and ever, and ever, and ever—

Above him, Terris frowned. Then his eyes went dark, then silver, and he bent down and whispered a single word in Miles's ear.

"*Seolfor.*"

A great rush came through Miles's body like a hard, hot wind, and the next thing he knew, he was bucking and shouting as he came, harder and hotter than he ever had in his life. What felt like gallons of cum shot out of him, onto his stomach, onto Terris, onto the sheets below. Flicks of white landed on Terris's still-swollen mouth, and it would have been beautiful. Except Terris had not come. His erection, in fact, had vanished. And he was looking down at Miles in terror.

"No," he whispered. He reached out and touched Miles's face hesitantly, all the while shaking his head. "No. *No.* It can't be. You cannot have gotten to him first!"

"What—?" Miles tried to ask, but he was too weak to finish the rest.

Terris's face shuttered, and he sat back, resting on his knees as he straddled Miles. He reached down and touched the ring in the center of Miles's necklace.

"Terris?" Miles whispered.

"Take him," Terris said, his voice not silky or loving, only hard and cold.

There was a bright, painful flash, and everything was gone. The castle, the bed, Terris—everything. Miles was still lying on his back, and he was still naked, but the ground beneath him was rough and hard, not soft. The air was not sweet with flowers and sun, but heavy and close, and it stank of death. It was pitch-dark too. Miles stilled, terrified, because he knew exactly where he was.

He heard the beast's hooves click against stone, and he whimpered as the hot breath fell, rank and putrid against his face.

Then the beast was gone, and a silvery ghost man stood in his place, Katie's silver ring glinting on his finger.

"*Know your heart*," the man said.

Then he vanished, and the beast returned in his place. It growled and reached for Miles.

Miles cried out—and the darkness was gone.

He lay naked in the leaves at the edge of the wood. He could hear the shouts of someone in the trailer park in the distance, and when he sat up, he could see the tops of some of the trailers. He looked down at himself and saw that he was naked, though he did have a string of hickeys across his chest and thighs. On a stump beside him were his clothes, folded neatly. His hat, scarf, and gloves were there too.

Scattered over the top of everything were the crushed, ruined petals of a white rose.

CHAPTER FIVE

Once I taste your honeyed wine,
once I see your glories shine,
once I am yours and you are mine,
then, sweet lover, I will be fine.

THE HOUR AFTER Miles had reappeared in the woods wasn't precisely pleasant.

After stumbling back into enough clothes to keep himself from getting arrested, he'd run back to the shop, where he had, as Patty put it, "raved like a loon, scared off all the customers, and taken six years off her life." She spent a solid half hour trying to calm him, then drafted her partner to help, but Julie had spent the whole time Miles had been gone in a meditation, and she was convinced that his danger was even greater than she'd first foreseen. She insisted they all go together to Katie's place right away, because Katie had studied magic longer—*magick*, she would say, with a *k*—and would hopefully know what to do.

And that was how Miles ended up sitting at Katie's

kitchen table, watching a beetle crawl across the wood as the three women argued in hushed but agitated tones in the dining room behind him.

He would have welcomed the rage he'd felt the last time he was here, because it would have been a great place to hide. But the rage was long gone, lost somewhere between leaving the trailer and the palace of the Lord of Dreams, and in its place was only an aching emptiness. The colors all around him were dull and lifeless, and even his friends' voices sounded discordant to his ears. Miles found his thoughts drifting back to Terris and the gleaming castle whenever he would let them, and these thoughts made him ache and yearn. It didn't matter that there was something disturbing about all of it, something that made him nervous and want to go lock himself in his room. It didn't matter, either, that all of this was absolutely crazy, seriously batshit crazy now. None of it mattered, not when he was thinking of Terris. When he thought of Terris, Terris was all that he wanted. It didn't matter that all of it had to be a dream. He wanted Terris any way he could get him.

The beetle was still crawling across the table, and Miles focused on tracking the insect to keep himself focused, though he also listened in increasing alarm to the snippets of conversation drifting through the closed door. The beetle was about a quarter inch long, fat as a dime, and it was black, though sometimes when it shifted it glinted a little. He wondered if its wings were doing that or if it had some sort of oil on its surface. He wondered, too, what kind it was. He'd seen it around his whole life, but he'd never bothered to figure out what it was called. It was just Some Black Beetle. Ugly, slightly gross, and it wandered across the table. Having spent several minutes exploring the classified section of a newspaper, it now wove its way to Miles.

"—should cast a few spells first, just to be sure. But I warn you, the stars are not aligned properly for this sort of thing. And I'm out of frankincense." Katie's voice cut through the door, and Miles hunched forward, holding his uneasy stomach. There was a high likelihood that soon he'd be drinking funky tea and sitting in the middle of a circle of candles wearing nothing but a towel draped around his waist, and knowing Katie, he'd have to beg to get that.

Because he'd been down this road, and he knew how this scene was going to play out—Katie would want to do a spell, Patty would make a face and say something scathing, and then Julie would give her a scolding look and point out that certainly it couldn't hurt. And Patty, though she would be thinking it was a bunch of nonsense, would concede Julie's point and not push because it wasn't *her* going to have to sit naked around hot wax, and because she didn't like to upset her wife. They'd done this to him when he'd first arrived, some charm or spell to "help him redirect his life." It had done absolutely nothing except embarrass the hell out of him.

There was no way this was going to end any other way, though. It was either going to be one of Katie's spell circles or a rehab clinic, because Patty was convinced Miles was high. Or insane. Or both. If Miles protested the spell, Patty would empathize, but she'd want to take him down to County Hospital. Which maybe was where he belonged.

Miles almost wished he *had* taken drugs, that this was all it could be. Because the alternative was far too surreal to contemplate.

He rested an elbow against the table and leaned heavily into his palm, watching glumly as the beetle crawled closer. "I don't want to be crazy," Miles told the insect. "But I don't want this to be real, either."

The beetle twitched its antennae at him, then turned and headed off to explore the wrapper of a blueberry muffin instead.

Miles sighed and went back to trying not to listen.

He didn't have to try long, because the next thing he knew the door opened and they came in. Patty crossed to the far side of the kitchen, where she folded her arms over her chest and leaned against the counter, looking cross. Julie came up beside her and stroked her arm, whispering soothingly.

Katie swept around the table with a flourish, her velvet skirt swishing and the beads on the hem of her shirt clinking as she sat down in the chair across from Miles. Her graying hair was thick and curling, but frizzy, and it reminded Miles of a dandelion gone to seed.

"So." Katie folded her arms over one another, tilted her head to the side and gave Miles a sad, knowing look. "We've had some trouble, haven't we?"

Miles turned to Patty. "Look, I've got enough money to go to the clinic and get an appointment. They'll give me, antidepressants, something to make me sleep, and an appointment with a counselor. I'm sure in a few weeks I'll be fine."

Patty wasn't appeased. "You came running into the shop half-naked, Miles. You were screaming and carrying on about some beast chasing you in the woods. And you were full of hickeys."

"There is something odd about your aura, Miles," Katie said, still speaking in lofty tones. "Even worse than that day you were in my shop. You are spiky and uneven all around. And yet in some places, it's like you aren't even here."

Miles blushed at the memory of stealing the ring, a reflection made worse by the fact that he'd lost it. But before he could offer to pay for it again, Katie was speaking once more.

"There's something going on with you, Miles. Something dangerous. You owe it to your friends and to yourself to discover what it is."

"For the last time—I wasn't with *anyone*. I fell asleep in the woods. I don't know how or why. I just woke up there. I had a weird dream." He saw the beetle poke its head out of the wrapper and had a fit of inspiration. "I bet the hickeys are bug bites. Please, Patty—I swear to God, I'm not on anything. I'll take whatever tox-screen you want."

Katie reached out and patted his hand, her lip bulging in an empathetic pout. "You poor thing. You just let Aunt Katie take care of you, hmm? We'll just check a few things, and then you can go home and drink some tea and get some sleep. Doesn't that sound nice?"

Julie came up beside Katie, her arms crossed and her hands tucked protectively against her sides. "Miles, your cards are very bad. And she's right. You have some strange energy around you. You need to let Katie cleanse you."

Miles cast a pleading look at Patty.

Patty stared back hard, worrying the side of her cheek with her teeth, but she just shook her head. "You weren't drunk, Miles, I know that, but you had to be on something. And you're not staying in my trailer if you're using. You can go shack up with whoever gave you your love bites."

Katie stood, scooped up the wrapper, beetle and all, and tossed it into the trash. "Come on into my workshop, sweetheart. It will only take a little while."

Miles cast one last pleading look to Patty, giving her his most innocent, most vulnerable look.

Fifteen minutes later, Patty and Julie were gone, and Miles was sitting naked in the center of a circle of white candles, a white washcloth over his groin as he listened to the dulcet whispers of Katie's spell.

Katie called to the four elements as she spread a ring of salt around the both of them, casting them inside with an altar. Miles also had his own circle inside the candles. It was cold in the room, and he had goosebumps.

Worst of all, though, was that Katie was naked too. It was for the purity of the spell, that much he knew, but it still unnerved Miles.

"I'm going to put you in a trance," she told him, setting down her bowl of salt and picking up a burning stub of sage. She sat down on her haunches and tilted her head to the side as she looked at him. "It's perfectly harmless, but by placing you inside the circle, it will make sure that if anything *does* go wrong, you'll be contained."

"You really think I'm dangerous?" Miles kept his eyes on her face. He'd tried looking at her knees, but then she'd shifted and given him a view he really, really didn't need. But when he saw how serious she was, he straightened. "Seriously—you think I am, don't you?"

Katie gave him a condescending smile. "Don't worry. We'll clean you up, just you watch." But there was a flicker of fear on her face too. She *was* scared.

And the fact that Katie was scared made Miles downright petrified.

Miles watched her continue closing the circle, chanting again, saying something about the four elements and the lords of each. Her fuzzy hair brushed her pale, freckled shoulders, and Miles stared at them to keep his gaze from drifting lower. But as he watched her move around the circle, her pale skin illuminated by the candlelight, he had a sudden flash back to a different set of shoulders in a different room, in a different light.

He had only remembered the dream in fragments, but now as he watched Katie move around the circle, it came back in a flood: Terris's shirt falling away. Terris's trousers sliding down his legs. Terris, gleaming and perfect, sliding his skin against Miles's own—

A faint clicking sound drew Miles partway back to reality. The black beetle from the muffin wrapper, or one of its cousins, skittered across the wood floor just outside the circle. Miles watched its antennae quiver and twitch, and he smiled at it in a daze.

The room began to fade, and Miles felt a momentary twinge of unease. Just as it had in the forest, the light began to change again. This time his unease was brief, and Miles quickly slid into a feeling of intense pleasure. He was dimly aware of Katie chanting on the other side of the circle of candles, but he was too focused on the increasing flood of sensory memory to pay her much attention. He could see Terris again, could feel him, could remember what it felt like to lie beneath him, what it was like to have Terris's body sliding over his own. Miles remembered the taste of him: his mouth, his skin, the tuft of hair above his cock. Katie's work room was disappearing, the dream castle returning. He could smell the summer wind drifting in through the open window, could smell the sun heating the silver velvet drapes.

He could feel the weight of silver necklace and the heavy press of the ring against his neck, so light, so sweet, *so tight*.

Something tickled against Miles's hand. He blinked, then gasped as a bright flash of light drew him abruptly back.

The castle vanished, and the circle of candles returned. The black beetle crawled over his hand, twitching over his ring finger, where the red ring of his burn was glowing with as much strength as it had four hours ago.

"Miles!" Katie was standing at the edge of the circle, staring at him, her face pale. She had a small sword in her hand. "Miles, what did you do?"

Miles blinked again. He felt dizzy, and his body felt heavy. "I don't know. You were chanting, and then—" The image of Terris flashed again, and Miles closed his eyes, sliding back into position with hardly any effort at all.

Another tickle, another flash, and he was back again.

"Miles!" Katie cried.

Miles's head was killing him. He displaced the beetle as he pressed his hand up against the side of his head as if to hold back the pain. "I don't know what's going on," he said, "but I don't like it. I want to get out of here."

"I think that's a good idea." Katie came forward with her hands raised. "Just hold still, and I'll undo the circle."

But when Katie started to chant again, the candles flared angrily. Miles watched the beetle pacing out the edge of the circle, lumbering determinedly over the ring of salt. When Katie frowned and began to chant again, the whole circle shuddered: the salt began to dance, bouncing against the floor as if there were an earthquake.

The beetle turned to Miles and twitched its antennae at him.

It swelled, suddenly growing as tall as Miles, and for a single second, Miles thought he saw a ghostly, silver-hued man smiling wryly at him. But only for a single second.

In the next second, the man burst into flame.

Miles cried out as the flames spread along the salt as if it were gunpowder, enclosing him inside its ring and licking at his skin, threatening to scorch him. He drew himself into a ball, but there wasn't much space for escape.

"Stop it, Katie!" he shouted. But Katie was shaking her head, wide-eyed, holding up her hands.

"I can't!" she shouted back. "I'm not doing anything! Miles, what the *fuck* have you been playing with?"

"A flute." Miles was beginning to sweat, both from the heat and from sheer panic at the realization that he was about to be burned alive. "That's all."

"It must be an enchanted flute," Katie said, eyeing the flames nervously.

"That's what I was thinking." Miles felt sick as he saw that the candles had melted away and now the flames were heading toward him, consuming the floor as they went. "Can't you throw something on this?"

"I'm afraid of making it worse," Katie confessed.

"Can I jump out of it?"

Katie bit her lip, then shrugged. "If it kills you, it will kill you faster, I suppose."

Miles rose unsteadily to his feet. He didn't even bother with the towel—at this point it almost seemed ridiculous. He made an attempt to smother part of the fire with it, but the towel went up as if it were made of paper. He didn't see what was going to keep the fire from burning him too.

Then he had a thought. "Katie, do you have those rose petals I found on my clothes?"

She broke the outside circle, crossed the room, then hurried back with them in her hand. "What do you want me to do with them?"

Miles had no idea. He rubbed his jaw and stared at the fire. "Throw them on the flames."

Katie tossed the petals into the air, and they both watched the white bits of flower drift down before crackling briefly.

Nothing happened.

Then, with a soft pop, the fire died. It disappeared

completely, going out as if someone had flipped a switch. The room went dark, too, but Miles didn't give a damn.

"It worked!" He laughed in nervous relief. "Katie, it worked!"

No one answered.

Miles turned around in the darkness, still inside the circle. "Katie?"

His voice sounded funny. It was echoing in a way that didn't fit the small workshop space.

Oh shit.

"Katie?"

A veil seemed to drop, invisible, but with it went the last illusion that Miles was still in southern Minnesota in a bossy and condescending Wiccan's workspace. He smelled damp and rot and dirt, and cold crept up around him like heavy fog.

Across the room a match flared, and Miles froze and watched, helpless, holding a candle aloft as the beast from the forest came forward, the *clop-clop* of his hooves echoing through the dungeon.

MILES STARTED TO back away, but the beast immediately stopped advancing and held up a hand.

"Stay," he said, his voice gruff. "You're safe where you are. I can't vouch for that if you leave the circle."

Miles looked down. There was indeed a circle around him: a blackened ring that looked the same as the scorch marks on Katie's floor, except that now it had a silver sheen to it, like dust. He looked back up at the beast, a thousand questions on his tongue, but fear held them all at bay.

"I won't hurt you," the beast said. "Not if you stay where you are."

Miles rubbed his arms, then lowered them quickly to his groin as he realized he was naked. Of course, so was the beast.

"Can you read my mind too?" he asked.

The beast gave a wry smile. "No. Just your face."

Miles studied the creature before him. He seemed less of an animal and more of a very hairy man who happened to have hooves for feet. It was the horns that grabbed Miles's attention. They were huge, fat things that started at the sides of his skull and curled back around his ears, the points curving up near either side of his jaw. They were the same brown as the hair that covered his body: hair on his head, his chin, his neck, his chest, shoulders, arms. It was less pronounced on his upper body, occurring more in patches and tufts, but once it hit his midsection, it was practically a pelt. It covered his waist, his legs—everything but his cock and his hooves, the latter which, Miles noted with some unease, were cloven.

The cock, too, was as big as it had been when it had flapped against the beast's leg as he chased after Miles, eager to rape him. Miles drew instinctively back.

"I'm not a devil," the beast said. "And I'm not your

enemy."

"But you'll attack me if I leave the circle," Miles finished, not quite certain this was fact yet, but it was confirmed when the beast nodded.

"Your spell has made a sort of a loophole to my enchantment," the beast said. "I am more man than beast while you remain inside that protective space." He gestured wryly at his body. "If you leave, you are subject to the same jurisdiction as me. The beast will take over, and at best, I'll be able to apologize as I tear you apart."

Miles shifted uneasily. "So you'll kill me?"

The beast looked shamefaced. "Not kill you precisely, though. I'd probably…take you by force, though. The beast would, anyway. I'm sorry."

Okay then. Miles wanted to shift, to scratch his arms and move to dislodge some of this nervous energy, but there was some strange psychological comfort to covering his genitals.

He cleared his throat instead. "So you're a *homosexual* beast."

The beast considered a moment, as if processing an unfamiliar word. He seemed to understand it but stumbled over speaking it. "No. I am a—" He paused, as if prepping his mouth. "—*homo-sexual* man. Or, I was. That's how I came here, of course."

"Oh?" Miles said, enticed by this new bit of information.

"Didn't you realize? You called to Him, in the forest, and he came to you. The Lord of Dreams. You were miserable, and you declared—from your heart— that you would do anything to escape your situation. And you are a man who desires men. You were like a perfect flower in a patch of weeds to him, and he plucked you."

"You mean Terris?" Miles asked, a hollow sense of loss expanding inside him. But the beast's face shuttered, and he shook his head.

"You must not speak of him to me."

That was what Terris had told him too. Which meant there was something important in that connection, and it also meant Miles had no way to explore it.

Yet.

"How did you come here?" Miles asked instead.

The beast shrugged. "I don't remember anymore. I don't think my home world even exists any longer. If it did, I wouldn't recognize it. I don't even know who or what I was before I was a beast." He rubbed at his chin with a hairy, clawed hand. "For a time I thought I had been a king, but very well this could be a fancy. I went mad long, long ago. There is very little man left, whoever he began as."

"You don't sound mad now," Miles pointed out.

"The loophole," the beast reminded him.

"Yes, but that doesn't explain how you got your sanity *back*."

The beast looked thoughtful. "That's true. I wonder how this is happening. A pity it won't be permanent."

"How do you know it won't?"

He tapped his horns, though Miles suspected he meant to simply indicate his head. "I can feel your circle pushing my enchantment back. When the circle is gone, I will return to my normal state, I'm sure." He frowned. "But you make a fair point. How am I affected by your circle when I stand without? I can only assume it is your magic."

Miles wanted to protest that he didn't have any magic, then decided it might be best to keep that information private. "What's your name?" Miles asked instead.

The beast laughed. "Oh, that's long, long lost."

That thought pained Miles somehow more than did hearing the beast couldn't remember his life. "But what should I call you?"

The beast shrugged. "It hardly matters. One way or another, we'll be lost to one another soon. You may select a name for me, if you wish."

Miles didn't wish, but he was distracted now by the rest of that statement. "Why will we be lost? What do you mean, one way or another?"

"You have been marked by the Lord of Dreams," the beast said patiently. "You will either succumb to Him and be consumed, or you will be outcast like me. Or you will waffle and become consumed by one of my kind. One way or another, this interview will be brief."

Miles didn't like the sound of any of this. "So you

refused this Lord of Dreams?"

The beast looked uncomfortable. "I cannot speak of that."

"Why not? How much worse can it possibly get for you?"

The beast averted his eyes. "He could start it all over. He could grant me back my sanity so that I could lose it again, only this time make it leave more slowly. He could give me to the other beasts, ones who are older and wilder." His hooves scuffed impotently at the floor. "It could be much, much worse."

"But I thought you refused him."

"There is no refusing the Lord of Dreams. There is only the surrender to His infinite pleasure, or there is the external pain that comes with clinging to one's own will."

Miles did not like any of this. "So I'm already doomed? That's what you're saying?"

The beast hesitated. "I haven't before seen anyone cast a circle and commune with an outcast." But his tone suggested this at best would only delay matters.

"I'm not gone yet," Miles said, a little desperately. "I suppose that was what Ter—that was what was going on at the castle, a seduction. But I wasn't seduced." He paused. "Wait—*wait*, that's it, isn't it? There was that part with the flower, where I forgot, but then he whispered something at the end, and I came—"

"Stop!" the beast whispered, alarmed.

Miles ignored him. "—and he said something. I

couldn't come until he said some word. But it wasn't one I knew."

"Sir, you must stop!"

Miles looked out at the beast's panicked face. "*Seol-for.*"

The circle shuddered, and the blackened circle around Miles burst into high flame again. The beast stepped back, but Miles stayed where he was and watched as the fire rose, then faded away again. The ring was brighter now. And when Miles looked closer still, he saw something lying inside it.

The flute.

He bent down and touched it tentatively, but it was cool to the touch. He picked it up and held it in his hand. Then he looked at the beast, questioning. But the beast wasn't looking at the flute, or even at Miles's face. He was looking at Miles's cock.

Miles started to cover himself again, then stopped as he got a better look at the beast's face. No one had ever looked at him like that. It was sexual, but the word seemed grossly understated. Carnal. Yearning. Aching, needing. He'd had men tell him they were going to worship his cock, but it had always been clearly a figure of speech. The beast was looking at him as the Biblical Adam must have looked at his Eve.

Or, in this case, his Steve.

Miles was flattered, but nervous too. "I suppose I could see how I could get drawn here. I haven't been very happy. I don't much like my life."

"Yes. That was much the way it was for me, this I do remember." The beast gave Miles a sad smile. "Trust me when I tell you that whatever your life is, it is better than what awaits you here."

Miles blushed, feeling foolish. "Why does it feel so good, if it's so bad?"

"Because He uses the echo of your dreams to lure you. He reaches into the dark parts of your heart, to the places where, like a child, you wish for what is not good for you to have."

Now Miles was angry. "Why is it so wrong to want happiness? Why can't I have good things in my life? Why does it have to be *this*?"

It sounded even more childish coming out of his mouth than it had echoing in his head, but that only served to frustrate Miles further. Naked, self-conscious, and confused, Miles waited for the beast to answer.

For a long time the beast only regarded Miles with his yellowed eyes, his countenance a mixture of terror and empathetic wisdom. Eventually he sighed.

"I couldn't have him," the beast whispered. "The man I wanted, I could not have him." He kept his eyes on Miles's cock as he spoke, softly, his voice aching with emotion. "I remember that much, as I look at you. I loved a man, but I could not have him. I don't know why anymore, but I remember that it made me ache. We frequently stood naked together for some reason, and it was then that I admired him, let my heart yearn. He was so beautiful. His shaft was unsheathed, like yours, and it was the first such I had ever seen. And I yearned for him with an intensity that I thought would kill me."

His lips parted, and he licked them so that they glistened, pale pink against the ruddy brown of his hair and rough skin. His eyes burned. "One night he was drunk, and he touched himself, and I watched. It was the most beautiful moment of my life, and I nearly died at the pleasure just of watching. In my delirium I called out that I would do anything, give anything, endure anything to have him. And that was how the Lord of Dreams came to me."

The beast fell silent, but there were particular details here Miles felt he had to know. "He came as the man you desired?"

"No." His reply was curt. "He came through my desire. It was another who came to me as the man I loved. But I cannot speak of that."

The intensity of the beast's gaze made Miles tremble and go soft all at once.

"Would you—would you touch yourself for me?" the beast asked.

Had he asked some other way—had he demanded, or asked politely, or tried to seduce him—anything else Miles was sure he would have refused or declined. But this was the ache he'd seen from Terris's sleigh. This was a soul-deep yearning.

This was a pain Miles knew intimately.

Miles reached down and took his soft penis tentatively in his hand. The beast shuddered, then growled, but he settled back on his hooves, watching. His eyes turned silver. He wanted this very much. He wanted this as much as he'd wanted that lover, Miles realized.

And something in Miles, something dark and cold and calculating whispered that this was an opportunity that would not readily come again.

Miles stroked himself, watched the silver sparkle, and asked, "What does the flute do?"

The beast's gaze did not leave Miles's cock. "It is his enemy. The flute is the Lord's enemy. We are not to speak of it. He will punish any who speak its name."

Miles paused. "He'll punish you now, just for that?" The beast nodded, and Miles took his hand away guiltily. This might be an opportunity, but he hadn't sunk so low as to punish someone who had clearly suffered more than his share of pain already.

The beast cried out. His eyes flickered as he shook his head. "Please—please, it will be worth it, to see you touch yourself for me. I will tell you anything if you continue."

"I don't want you to get hurt!"

"Some pleasure is worth great pain."

Miles began to stroke himself again, tentatively, but he was light-years away from arousal now. He couldn't make the beast tell him about the flute, not if it was going to hurt him. But if he didn't learn *some* answers, his goose was as cooked as the beast's.

Maybe you can save him, too, if you figure this out.

Surely that was wishful thinking. The whole thing might be.

But if he didn't risk this, what else was there to do? Katie was no help, and Julie had already said this was over her head. If Patty couldn't shoot it or shout at it, she was lost. Even if there were someone in his world who could come to his aid, Miles didn't know how to find them, and he suspected he wouldn't have time. This beast was it.

"I'm going to try to fight this," Miles said. "And if I can, I'll try to help you too."

The beast smiled sadly. "You cannot help me. But it is kind of you to offer."

Miles nodded, trying not to feel sick. "Then I'll alleviate your suffering as much as I can. Even if it's to give you pleasure. So that's the bargain. I'll ask you questions, and then I will give you whatever pleasure you ask for. Obviously I can't leave the circle, but whatever I can give you from here, I will."

The beast looked up at Miles's face. His eyes were completely silver now, flickering like a banked fire. "Whatever I ask?"

What a horrible existence, Miles thought, that he would endure endless suffering just to see someone jack off. He nodded. "Anything. For as long as you like."

The beast shook his head. "No. If you grant me that, I'll keep you here forever."

"I don't know how to leave," Miles pointed out.

The beast nodded to the flute. "It will take you anywhere you want to go."

Miles looked down at the flute, then back at the beast. "Anywhere?"

The beast held out his hands. "I accept your bargain. Please, sir—ask me anything."

"My name is Miles," Miles said quietly.

The beast made an awkward bow. "It is my pleasure to meet you, Miles. Now please ask me what you will, and I will answer honestly, I swear on my honor."

Whoever you were, you were a man with honor, Miles thought. He tilted his head to the side and considered the beast a moment.

"Will you be offended if I call you Harry?"

The beast smiled. "Not at all. Harry I am, from this point on."

Miles nodded. "Okay. Harry, can the flute help me escape the Lord of Dreams?"

"Yes," Harry said, "if he who plays it knows how to use it."

"Do *you* know how to use it?"

Harry shook his head.

Miles looked down at the flute, flicking his thumb over the mouthpiece as he considered. "I wish I knew how I came by it."

"It comes to everyone who is called by the Lord of Dreams," Harry said. "But no one has yet figured out how to use it to escape."

"Can you call it too?" Miles asked. Harry shook his

head. Miles frowned down at the flute. "What's the difference between me and you, then?"

"He's still seducing you," Harry said. "He has already cast me out. But He has His imprint on me still, you see. That's what happens. Once you look at Him, you cannot leave Him, even if you refuse Him. Part of you will want Him."

"So I just have to keep from looking at him?"

Harry shook his head. "You can't."

"Even with the flute?" Miles turned it over in his hand. "I imagine someone's already tried playing it at him?"

"Oh yes, often."

"And?"

"Generally He rips them in pieces and throws them to the beasts. But every now and again, He's more creative. Once He made a challenger who played the flute at Him part of a show, keeping him alive while each of the beasts raped him. That went on for a long, long time before He grew bored."

Miles tried not to think about that. "There's a funny tone in your voice when you talk about him. You sort of hesitate, even just to say 'he.' Like he's God."

"To me, He is." Harry shrugged, but sadly. "He imprisoned my desires. I hate Him, but I love Him. He is, as He is to all men, everything we want, everything we crave."

"But that was Terris," Miles insisted, and the silver went out of Harry's eyes.

"No," he said gruffly. "I still cannot speak of him."

"But why not?" Miles demanded, frustrated at this impotence.

"No," Harry said again, and nothing more.

Miles considered this. "But you have said—and he said—that he and this Lord are not one and the same. Can you at least confirm that?"

Harry nodded reluctantly.

He looked exquisitely uncomfortable and spoke no more. But Miles read his face, and what he saw there said that whatever was between Harry and Terris was bigger, even, than this Lord of Dreams. Who was, as far as Miles could tell, God to them both. By definition, nothing could be bigger than God. Which meant this was a paradox.

Miles couldn't decide if that was good or bad.

He rubbed his thumb absently against the flute. "Will He appear to seduce me?"

Harry nodded. "Eventually."

"So Terris is like foreplay?"

Harry said nothing. Miles rubbed his thumb harder against the flute and gnawed on his bottom lip as he tried to process all these pieces in his head. Everything about Terris was off-limits with Harry. That wasn't going to be helpful. He tried to think of how to re-phrase.

"Why haven't I been lured in yet?"

Harry shrugged, looking a little easier. "Impossible to say. It could be His will."

"And it could be mine," Miles said.

Harry nodded, then said no more.

"How did *you* succumb to him?"

Harry paused. His eyes strayed to Miles's cock again, and Miles took this to mean Harry's answer would cost him great pain, and that he was reminding himself of what that pain would buy. Miles tried not to feel guilty.

"As He does to all men who come to Him, he presented Himself to me as perfection, as all I could ever want in a man. He made exquisite love to me and offered me the ultimate, eternal pleasure, if only I would give myself—and my will—to Him. I wanted Him as I have wanted nothing else." His face grew dark. "But... the other came. He... complicated things. And after him, I could not yield my will to the Lord, not for my pleasure nor for his and not even to end my suffering. And so He ordered my pride to consume me for all eternity, keeping me near to Him but refusing to allow me into His Paradise."

This speech was delivered matter-of-factly, with a hint of resignation and humility to it, too. But there was something else in there, something unsaid. Something important.

Miles tried to find the way to press on it. "Is your punishment similar to that of many others, then?"

Harry paused. The tension in his expression told Miles all he needed to know. This was a very *special* sort of pain.

"Never mind," he said, relieving him. "But I have a different question—why have I only seen you and not any of the other beasts?" Another thought struck him. "Wait—why do I see you at all? Why are you here, now? Where are we? How is this happening?"

It was too many questions, he knew, but there was a thrill of something pulsing inside him now, the sense of an answer nearly found, or at least a big pile of mess which, if sorted out, might truly give him some of the answers he was seeking. He waited, breathless, watching Harry's every expression, determined to glean whatever information he could. And what he learned was that these questions, either in whole or in part, were a great stress to Harry. He looked almost sick, so much so that Miles gave in and held up a hand.

"You don't have to tell me," he reminded him gently.

Harry shut his eyes a moment. His bulky shoulders dropped, and he looked ashamed. "I want—I want to see you. I must pay for that."

"No." Miles held out his hand. "I'll give you that regardless."

Harry opened his eyes. "You don't have to do that. I don't deserve that."

Miles felt a pang, an ache that pierced him like an arrow. "You deserve a lot more than that. Because whatever you did or didn't do in your life, you don't deserve this."

"How do you know?" Harry whispered. "I might

have been a monster."

"You aren't now," Miles said. "I don't care what your outside looks like. You're a good man. And that man is still in there, after all this time."

Miles realized as he spoke the words that they were true. After only God knew how many years of suffering, of madness, of pain. When all that was stripped away, Harry was kind and gentle and good, beautiful in a way that had nothing to do with his outside. This realization shamed Miles in a way that no lecture from Patty or Katie ever could. "I don't deserve the help you're giving me. You're so much better than I am. *You* deserve to get out of here. I should have to stay down here in this pit and learn to grow up."

Harry looked pained. "No. Do not say such things. No one deserves this. No one."

"I'm going to save you," Miles vowed in a whisper. "I'm not going to rest until I do. No matter what it costs me. No matter how hard it is."

Harry reached for him, his expression soft, then stopped as he recalled the barrier of the circle. He lowered his hand, but he stepped as close as he could to the edge.

"You will save me, Miles," he said quietly, "by saving yourself."

Miles's emotions threatened to overwhelm him, and he stood rigid for almost a full minute as he tried to tamp them back down. When his will did not suffice, he began to rub his thumb against the flute again and found his despair begin to bleed away.

"Is there anything else you can tell me to help me?" he asked Harry when he was able to speak again.

Harry's face clouded. He neither nodded nor shook his head, his face wooden once more.

There was something huge here, Miles knew, something he wasn't comprehending. He rubbed the side of his head with his free hand, then sighed. "I can't think anymore. It's all jumbled in my mind."

"Perhaps reflect on it in private," Harry suggested.

Miles nodded, but he felt grim. Would he see Harry again—the man, not the beast? Would he have to run from him in the forest?

Would he see Terris? Or would his next round be with this Lord of Dreams?

Miles lifted the flute and studied it for a moment, as if perhaps it might have the answers he sought. Then placed the flute carefully on the floor.

"Thank you for your help. I'll do my best to use it wisely." He held out his hands to his sides, displaying his body. "Now I'm yours. What will you have me do?"

Harry's eyes darkened again. His eyes drifted over Miles hungrily. "It's enough to look at you," he said, but there was longing in his voice.

"Harry, I've given you license to have anything that you want. I'd give you more if I were able. You can only look, though, so you're going to have to tell me: what is it you want to see?"

Harry looked him in the eye. "Anything? Anything

at all?"

"Anything," Miles said.

Harry hesitated. Then his eyes burned silver, and when he spoke, his voice was rich with lust. "Turn around, Miles."

He worried that Harry would turn into a beast if Miles aroused him too much, but he pushed that fear aside. He owed this much to Harry. For helping him, and for simply enduring what he had been through. For being the man, even as a beast, that Miles had never managed to be.

Taking a deep breath and gathering his courage, Miles turned around, showing his backside to Harry, and waited for what was next.

CHAPTER SIX

Your lips, your breast

your slender chest

your every glance, your very breath—

I want you, lover, for my death.

F OR SEVERAL SECONDS, Miles simply stood there, feeling awkward, slightly nervous, and very aroused. He wondered if this would be it, if Harry would just want to look at him. He remembered the story Harry had told earlier, about the man he'd wanted and how he hadn't even touched him. He wondered if his performance might overload Harry, something as raw as this after all this time, and if Harry wouldn't be able to say anything at all. Miles decided if Harry didn't take control, he'd turn around and try to masturbate himself for him. He owed him that much.

"Bend over and grab your ankles, so that you are open to me."

The command, abrupt and slightly rough, surprised Miles. He could hear the beast in that order, mixing in with Harry the man.

Miles flexed his hands a few times, let out as much of his tension as he could on a breath, and slid his hands down his thighs, over his knees, then bent all the way forward and grabbed his ankles. Then he waited.

He could feel his hole open—not much, really, but enough that he knew Harry had a pretty X-rated view. For a long time, Harry said nothing, but Miles could hear him breathing, almost huffing as he stared at Miles's upturned ass and open thighs. When it went on a little longer, Miles dared to peek between his legs, and started as he saw Harry standing very close to the edge of the circle, legs apart, one clawed hand reaching down to stroke his long, rapidly hardening cock.

Miles averted his eyes and shut them a moment, but only saw the monster cock lingering there in his head, and then opened his eyes again, staring intently at the silver ring around the circle.

"Reach up and spread yourself more open." Harry's voice was so gruff now that it was almost a growl. "Show me your channel, Miles."

Miles was breathing harder, and he was aroused, but at that last part, he had to smile. "Channel?" he repeated, as he slid his hands back up toward the backs of his thighs.

Harry grunted. "That isn't what you call it?"

Miles frowned. "Harry, you must be from my world, if you speak English."

"The enchantment translates it for us, I suspect."

"Why would your enchantment—your punishment—help you understand me?"

"Not my enchantment. Yours."

"No," Miles said, very confused now. "That makes *no* sense. Why would this Lord guy make it easier for you to understand me, when you're helping me—"

"Show me your channel, Miles!"

It was a rough command, but there was panic in there too. *I've gotten close again*, Miles realized. Too close.

He reached up and placed his hands on either side of his cheeks. "It's an ass," he said. "Asshole. You say, 'Show me your asshole, Miles.'"

"That is vulgar," Harry said.

Miles laughed. "Well, *yeah*." He glanced over his shoulder at Harry. "But if you'd rather, we can call it my pucker. Or my 'rosebud,' but I hate that one. 'Opening' works, I guess. Or 'anus'."

"Miles?"

"Hmm?" Miles said, startled out of his muse.

Harry leveled a hot gaze at him. "Show me your asshole, Miles."

Miles grinned and spread his cheeks.

His knees went a little weak at the look that Harry gave him. Miles knew he wasn't ugly, but he didn't have the kind of looks men went stupid over. He could usually get somebody to take home or to go home with if he cruised, but nobody had ever worshipped him. Not like Harry did now. Anybody watching the two of them would have thought Miles was some sort of

Madonna that Harry had waited his whole life to kneel down before. His jaw was slack, his eyes unfocused and yearning, his whole upper body quaking as he stroked himself furiously.

All this just from Miles pulling his ass open.

"So beautiful," Harry whispered. "Would that I could touch it. I would kiss your opening, Miles. I would bury my face inside your musk, and I would thrust inside you until I made you moan."

He wasn't far from that now, Miles conceded. He shut his eyes and took a breath, steadying himself. Then he let go with one hand, drew his fingers to his mouth and sucked two of them hard, getting them very, very wet before reaching back around, opening himself again, and this time pressing the tip of one of his fingers up against his asshole.

"Oh yes," Harry called out hoarsely. "Oh yes. Oh yes. Push it inside, Miles. *Oh yes.*"

Miles did, sucking in a breath as he impaled himself. He felt dizzy, both with arousal and with the heady thrill that came with knowing how much he affected Harry. He found he kept forgetting that the other man was almost a monster, especially now that he wasn't looking at him. In his mind's eye, he saw a tall man with a beard, looking slightly medieval and very big, very buff—not Miles's type at all, not anything like Terris, but none of that mattered right now. Right now was this weird, tense moment, filled with questions that led to more questions and paradoxes and contradictions, and right now he was giving Harry pleasure. This moment was all for Harry.

Miles pushed his finger deeper and smiled as Harry groaned.

He fucked himself slowly, trying to think of everything that had ever turned him on in the masturbatory videos he'd taken to watching online since coming home. He remembered the one of the young man who had boldly climbed onto his bed, bent over onto his knees, and proceeded to slow-fuck himself, taking every viewer who logged on to a jaw-aching climax with nothing more than two of his own fingers. Miles played the video over in his mind a few moments, remembering.

Then he sank to his knees, opened his knees wide, braced his head against the floor, reached behind and did his best to recreate it.

Harry approved. He made several lusty barks, urging Miles to push deeper, *harder*, and Miles did, but remembering the magic of that hot young slut, he kept it maddeningly slow. When he began to excite himself to the point that he lacked control, he regained some ground by crying out, and when he found how much Harry liked the sounds he made, he made more of them, letting himself go until he was practically an animal too.

When it became too much, he slid one hand back around and began to tug urgently at himself.

"No!" Harry barked, and Miles stopped and lifted

his head.

"What did I do?" he asked.

"Turn over," Harry growled. "Onto your back, and spread your legs. Let me see you. Let me watch you pleasure yourself."

Miles rolled over. By accident he brushed against the edge of the circle and felt a sharp *hum* against his skin, as if he'd run into electricity. He slid away, back to where Harry could get a good look at him, then lay on his back, drew his legs up against his chest, and smiled as he watched Harry become undone all over again.

He spit into his palm, then began to work himself again, using one hand to play with his balls and occasionally sneak down to work inside as he tugged at himself, insistently now, not slow in the slightest, just rough, raw masturbating and—he gasped as he opened his leg and gave himself room and thrust inside—fucking.

"Harry," Miles gasped, shutting his eyes and imagining the burly, hairy, handsome man Harry was becoming in his mind pushing his legs back and taking him. "Harry!"

"I'm here," Harry rasped. He was grunting rhythmically, and when Miles dared a look, he saw that Harry was working himself just as hard, aiming that gigantic cock at the circle, stroking it furiously as he kneaded his balls and kept his eyes on Miles. Miles met his stare, let himself merge the idealized Harry with the real man-monster that stood before him, and then, with barely any warning, rolled his eyes back and exploded with a cry that bounced off the stone walls and rang in his ears.

He heard an echoing bellow, then felt something hot and wet splash across his body. Dizzy, he looked up in time to see one last arc of cum spray across the silver line to land on Miles's exposed ass and on his still-quivering belly.

Then he realized what had happened, and what that meant, and from the look on Harry's face, he saw that he had seen it too.

Miles held his breath as Harry, hand shaking, reached out and into the circle.

It snapped, popped, and pushed him back.

Miles felt a swift ache of loss. He pushed up onto his elbows, watching Harry, wanting him. He swallowed against a dry throat and said, "Harry—"

But Harry's head jerked up, and though Miles saw and heard nothing, Harry's face became alarmed. "You must go," he said. "Go back. Take the flute. Use it wisely."

Miles sat up. "But I don't want to leave you, not like this—"

"You must go."

Miles stood, holding the flute. "I'm coming back for you."

Harry shook his head. "It won't be me. It will be the beast. Go, and forget me, Miles. Go and set yourself free."

I'm going to set the both of us free, Miles thought, then lifted the flute to his lips and played.

Harry and the dungeon vanished, and Katie, now fully clothed, reappeared. She was screaming.

"I WANT THE whole story this time." Katie poured Miles a shot of vodka into a glass before taking a hit for herself straight from the bottle. "I want to know where you went when you left the circle. I want to know how you got there. I want to know how you got back." She took another hit, then winced and shook her head. "I do *not* need to know why you have dried spunk all over you."

Miles downed the shot and wrapped the blanket she'd brought him tighter around his body. He was dressed now, but he couldn't shake the feeling of cold. "I'm not sure where I went, but I've sort of been there before. I went there when I first started hallucinating— when I found that website."

"Website?" Katie echoed.

Miles told her about the flute showing up at the pawn shop, about his Google searches, and about the strange way the room flickered in and out of Harry's dungeon. Katie listened, tapping the side of the bottle with her fingernails.

"And you clicked on this site that said Terris something or other," she repeated when he finished, "and you found that by searching for 'magic flute.'"

"Yes." Miles glanced at the flute, which was lying on the table between them. "And Terris is the man who found me in the forest when I wandered in there without meaning to."

"Who carried you off in a sleigh that just sort of skipped over the leaves and tree stumps, while a horned beast who wanted to rape you tried to catch up. Who made love to you in a castle, then said some word and you came back, only to end up with the beast while in my circle, where you gave him a little sex show as thanks for giving you absolutely no answers to any questions. Oh, and for some reason there he was articulate and almost gentlemanly. Did I miss anything?"

Miles thought a moment, but he didn't even stop to acknowledge how crazy it all sounded. He was numb to almost everything now. "I think you hit the high points."

Katie shook her head. "You know, I really did think you were using. I was just going to sweat it out of you, maybe hypnotize you and get me to tell me what you took. If I hadn't seen you vanish with my own eyes, I still wouldn't believe you."

"But you believe me now?" Miles asked, hating how much he wanted her to. He still didn't like her, but damn, he needed an ally here. Anywhere. The ache was coming back again, the yearning to return to the Lord of Dreams, or to Terris, or something—he ached, and he knew enough now to know he needed to resist that siren call. He'd hoped the alcohol would distract him, but it was only lowering his inhibitions, making the ache worse.

He couldn't seem to stop drinking, though, and he knocked back a second shot when Katie poured him one, then gave herself another hit as well.

Katie sighed. "I don't know what I believe anymore, Miles. I do think something weird is going on. I'm holding off on judgment as to whether or not some sex-crazed Lord of Dreams is trying to draft you into his man-harem."

"Can't we look this up, or something?" Miles pressed. "Find out who this is and how to get out of it?"

Katie snorted. "Look it up where? This isn't *Buffy the Vampire Slayer*. No Giles and no Codex. And given what happened to you when you tried a Google search, I'm counting that out, too."

Miles glared at her. "So you're just committing me to death?"

"If you keep whining? Yes." She picked up the flute and turned it over a few times in her hands. "This is his enemy, is it? Awfully inanimate."

"I was hoping you would maybe recognize it," Miles admitted. "It's magic, and you do magick." Funny. He was starting to *hear* that extra k.

Katie lifted her eyebrows. "Miles, magick is ninety percent philosophy. There is no Hogwarts and no gingerbread house."

"And no Codex." Miles took the flute back from

her and stared at it. "But what am I supposed to do with it?"

"You said the monster—"

"Harry," Miles corrected sharply.

Katie rolled her eyes. "Your boyfriend Harry the monster said the flute would take you wherever you wanted to go. I think that's a good start, don't you?"

"But I don't know where I want to go!" He threw up his hands in frustration. "All I know is that I need somewhere with actual answers. But I don't know where that is."

"You could start there," Katie suggested. "Just say 'take me somewhere with actual answers.' Couldn't hurt."

"I could cut to the chase," Miles said. "Go right to this Lord guy."

Katie frowned. "It does seem odd that this Lord of Dreams selected you but you haven't met him. You'd think he'd be a bit more invested. Unless Terris is doing his work for him."

"I thought that, too, but it's endearing me to Terris, not this Lord of Dreams."

"Maybe he's bored and wants a threesome," Katie suggested wryly.

Miles drummed his fingers on the table. "I swear the key to this is that Terris and Harry freak out when I talk to one of them about the other. I just wish I knew why. If I could get the flute to take me to *that* answer, I'd be set."

Katie passed the flute back to him. "Go back to Patty and Julie's house and get something to eat. Sleep if you can."

Miles stared at her. "That's *it*? That's all you've got? 'Go to bed'?"

Katie pursed her lips. "Miles, this isn't logical. It doesn't fit anything I know of magick, and I know *all* about magick."

"So—what, I just hang out while you study up?" he shot back. "In the Codex that doesn't exist?"

She said nothing, just nudged the flute harder at his arm.

Miles took it and rose. He crossed the room and put on his coat, frustrated, and slightly panicked too. But as he did up his zipper, his eyes caught something glinting on the table—one of Katie's silver scoops—and he paused.

"Silver," he said out loud. He turned back to Katie. "Everything is silver with this. The sleigh, the decorations at the castle—everything is silver." He blushed. "And the ring that I stole. I'm sorry for that, again. For losing it."

Katie waved his apology away with a weary sigh. "It was maybe worth ten bucks on a good day, because it was only silver-plated. But you're right, silver is decidedly a theme." She brushed her hands together in a dismissive fashion. "I'll study it for you."

But Miles's mind was still whirring. "The flute is silver too. And the flute is the Lord's enemy. So does that mean he hates music, or a metal?" Miles sighed. "I so suck at this."

Katie patted his shoulder. "Go sleep." She reached into a box on a shelf and handed him a small cloth bag. "And keep this in your pocket. Keep it closed, too, and bring it back for me to refresh on the next full moon. It will keep any bad influences away."

Miles wasn't so sure a bag was going to do anything like that, but he took it anyway, tucking it into the pocket of his jeans. He still didn't know how he was going to solve this, and he brooded on it all the way back to the trailer park. He had to walk again, but this time he took the long way around, not letting himself get anywhere near the forest. By the time he got to the double-wide, it was almost dark. It was cold too. He'd never fully warmed up from earlier, and now the wind blew through his clothes, making him shake. When he opened the door, the warmth and the smell of Julie's soup wrapped around him and pulled him quickly inside.

Both Patty and Julie were there, and they eyed Miles nervously.

"Katie called," Patty said carefully. "She said you weren't using. She swore you weren't, in fact."

Julie's eyes were wide. "And she said you're the prince in some fairytale?"

Patty snorted and rolled her eyes.

Miles slumped into his chair. "I'm more like the dumb guy who bumbles around." He helped himself to soup and bread, but he didn't eat, just poked his spoon into his bowl. Patty studied him for a few moments, then went back to her own meal.

Julie beamed at Miles. "Well, I think it's exciting, and it makes perfect sense with your cards. But be careful, Miles. You have a lot of danger ahead of you."

Miles thought of the man with ten swords in his back and pushed his bowl away.

After dinner, he went with Patty back to the pawn shop to help her sort through an estate sale she'd bought some things from. Normally he hated this sort of thing, but tonight he was ready to take any excuse not to deal with his problems. And he was frankly terrified of going to sleep. When he saw what they had to mark and stock, he realized this would be no problem.

"This is a lot of stuff," he said when he saw the storeroom.

Patty nodded and cracked into the first box. "I want to get into some antiques. Figured this is a good way to start."

"Really?" Miles raised his eyebrows. "You? Antiques?"

Patty shrugged, self-conscious. "Always liked them. Made everything look nice without being cold. They look stupid in a trailer, though, so I thought maybe if I sold them it'd be kind of a compromise."

Miles tried to imagine Patty in a house full of antiques. It worked oddly well. "You should get an old house," he said. "And fix it up. It could even be your shop."

"No money. Can't get a loan. No clue how to fix stuff like that. Not to do it right." She picked up a dirty, broken doll and grimaced before tossing it into the trash can beside her. "It's just a dream that didn't work out. Same damn story as everybody else."

Patty wanted to run an antique shop. He could see it all the clearer the more he thought of it, this shop that would never be, and it made him sad. And he felt embarrassed, the same as he'd felt with Harry. He'd never thought about Patty having a dream like this. He'd never once considered that she was living any-thing other than the life she'd chosen, than the life she'd wanted.

He'd never once considered that maybe part of her was pining after her own Atlanta too.

Miles looked around at the assorted junk. It wasn't very antique-like.

"We could get to some sales some weekend," he said. "Borrow a truck from somebody. I'd be happy to help you." He looked up at her. "And—well, if things turn around enough for you to find some house to fix up, *I* know how to do all that stuff. Some of the plumbing you want to hire out for, but not much. I could do the rest."

Patty gave him a sidelong look, then shook her head. "You sure it wasn't aliens grabbed you, not some dream guy? Reprogrammed your brain to make you stop whining and want to help me?"

Miles tilted his head to the side and smiled at Patty. "Are you complaining?"

She smiled back, shook her head, and handed him a box. "Here."

They worked for several hours, talking a little, but mostly just working. Patty shed her flannel and worked in her muscle T, and Miles shoved up his sleeves, finally finding warmth at last. When they had the whole place sorted, it was late, and they were tired. But Miles felt good. He still felt the ache for Terris and the Lord of Dreams, but the ache had diminished now, tempered by good, hard work.

"Thanks," Patty said, handing him a beer when they were back in the trailer. She toasted him and added, "Hope the Prince of Darkness doesn't kidnap you overnight."

"Lord of Dreams," Miles murmured, but his stomach ached a little at the thought of going to sleep.

He drank his beer in front of the TV, but when his head began to nod, he went to his room, turned on all the lights, and began to pace.

Should he just go to sleep? Would it be okay? Or should he try to go somewhere with the flute? He picked up the instrument several times, but the timing didn't feel right. He ended up lying on his bed, fully dressed, staring up at the ceiling, thinking furiously. There had to be some way the flute could help. He could feel it. He just had to think of the right answer….

When he fell asleep, he hardly noticed. One minute he was thinking of how to use the flute, and the next minute he was flying, soaring high above the trailers, above the road, the field, and then, inevitably, above the trees. He saw the clearing below, and he smiled as he came down, feeling the summer wind rush around him, smelling the sweet summer air.

He saw the silver glint even before the sleigh, and he was running even before he hit the ground.

Terris, white and gleaming in the moonlight, smiled at him.

"Hello, darling." He opened his arms.

Miles, caught up in the spell, smiled back, embraced him, and bent his head back to receive his lover's kiss.

I'M DREAMING, MILES thought, absently, as Terris took his lower lip between his teeth. He groaned. *It's a fucking good dream.*

"Darling," Terris murmured. He took Miles's face between his hands and deepened the kiss briefly. "Darling, we cannot linger here. Let me take you somewhere very special."

Miles, dream-groggy, only nodded and snuggled in against Terris's shoulder as Terris took the ribbon-reins and aimed them deeper into the woods. The trees sped by in a blur, but Miles paid them no attention, too busy trying to undo the silver frogging on Terris's jacket and wriggle his way inside.

Terris laughed, a wicked, satisfied sound. He kissed Miles's temple, letting his tongue steal out to lick his skin. "So eager for me? Don't worry, love. I won't disappoint you this time."

You couldn't ever disappoint me, Miles wanted to say, but then his fingers found the buttons of Terris's shirt, and Terris helped him find his skin, and once Miles had his sights on his lover's dusky nipple, he would have nothing else. Terris hissed, then murmured his encouragement as he buried his fingers in Miles's hair, keeping him firmly in place.

"That's it, Miles," Terris whispered. He put the reins in the hand at Miles's head and used the other to further reveal the landscape of his smooth, flat chest. "Taste me. I am yours, lover. All yours."

Miles did—he tasted every exposed inch of Terris's flesh, lapping at his skin as if it were the only meal he had seen in a week. He felt that ravenous for his lover—he felt as if he'd die if he didn't have him, as if he would give anything at all to taste him, touch him, take him inside. When he was with Terris, the yearning narrowed, but it sharpened too. *This.* This was what he needed. What he wanted. Terris was all that there was in the world.

The sleigh stopped at the edge of a glistening pond edged with lush grasses and flowers. Huge willow and birch trees circled the water, bending over it and creating a green and silver canopy over a bed of white petals arranged in a fragrant patch just wide enough to bear the bodies of two men. Miles barely remembered leaving the sleigh: one minute he ran his tongue along a tight cord in Terris's neck, and the next he pressed him into sea of white, taking in tiny bits of rose as he continued his way down Terris's naked shoulder. They were both naked now, and Terris's hands skimmed over Miles's bare hips, kneading softly at the flesh of his backside.

"Make love to me, Miles." A finger pressed at Miles's entrance, and Miles groaned and pushed against it, sucking it into the heat of his ass. Terris pushed deep, then flicked his tongue over Miles's nipple. "Put your cock inside me, darling. Take me any way you like. Claim me. Take me here inside this beautiful dream. Fill me up. Ride me, Miles, to your pleasure—to both our pleasures."

"I will," Miles said, but he groaned as Terris pushed deeper, wanting more. If only there were a way they could fuck each other at the same time."

"Oh, if that's all you want," Terris purred. He withdrew his finger, and Miles cried out in disappointment, but mere seconds later he gasped and spread his legs as something smooth and slick and *cold*, fucking *cold* worked its way inside him. He grunted as it grew wider, but he opened for it, panting and urging Terris incoherently to push it in, to plow him deep. For several minutes, this is just what Terris did, until Miles huffed and thrust back against the phallus, driving himself to the brink. Terris buried it deep, wrapped a silver belt around Miles's waist, and tied it tight. Then he knelt on the ground before Miles and presented him his perfect, puckered ass.

"Fuck me, Miles," Terris gasped. He circled his hips invitingly. "Fuck me while it fucks you."

Miles rose up, aimed himself, and drove home. Terris was already well-greased—it was a dream in every way, apparently—and he slid straight in to the hilt. Terris was so hot, so tight, and so perfect that Miles shook, crying out his incoherent bliss before the need possessed him and he began to thrust. He shouted in happy surprise as the phallus Terris had strapped to him began to fuck him too; Miles braced against Terris's hips and humped like a dog, torn between the joyous sensation of Terris's ass and the monster in his own. *It's so big*, he thought, and without warning had a vision of Harry's great cock, thrusting in and out of his hand.

Beneath him, Terris stiffened. "Wait—*no!*"

But it was too late. Miles roared, and with the image of Harry plowing him roughly shaking his mind, he came hard, filling Terris with his cum. When he finished, he fell off him and onto the petals, still twitching and moaning from the thrill of the phallus inside him.

Harry. Oh, Harry.

Terris leapt on him, but not in lust; he grabbed Miles's shoulders and bore down on him, his face twisted in rage.

"You're ruining *everything!*" he shouted, and Miles

just looked up at him in confusion as the dream began to fade and he found himself back in his room once again.

He was lying naked on his bed, which was full of white rose petals. There was the distinct pressure of something hard and huge in his ass, and when he reached down for it, he felt the belt Terris had tied, and with a gasp and a grunt, he pulled out the phallus Terris had put there.

It was silver.

CHAPTER SEVEN

Do not let me face my past.
Hold me close and hold me fast.
Tie my body to the mast.
Let me see only pleasure everlast.

MILES DIDN'T TELL Katie or anyone else about the dream. He gathered up every last rose petal in a garbage bag and hid it in his closet, and he put the silver phallus in a drawer with his underwear. After that, he simply got dressed, ate breakfast with Julie, then headed over to work with Patty. He worked hard, helping her as much as he could, but it was not out of a desire to please or to thank her. He worked to escape.

If he didn't think about it, he told himself for the thousandth time as he unpacked the last of the estate sale boxes, then it would go away. If he just kept himself busy, if he didn't think about silver or sleighs or the perfect way Terris tasted or the way his heart had lifted up when he thought of Harry pressing him down into the petals, kissing him deeply as he rubbed their cocks together—

Falling forward and resting his forehead against an unopened crate, Miles admitted his strategy was not only dubious, it wasn't working. He was thinking about Terris and Harry all the time now.

The only way he didn't think of them was to murmur out loud like a madman, "Don't think about it. Don't think about it. Don't think about it." If he did that and imagined a big black square, he could drag himself off course for about fifteen minutes, tops.

He was so fucked.

Julie noticed that he was upset, but Miles deflected all her concerns. It wasn't that he didn't want help. He just didn't want to go back to Katie's again, because her "go to sleep" strategy *so* did not work, and neither did her charm, which Miles had eventually just thrown away. Julie couldn't help him either. No one could.

But once Patty was in bed that night, Julie came back out to the TV room where Miles was trying to think about the evening news instead of Terris and failing miserably. She curled up on the couch beside him and said nothing, just reached out and took his hand.

Miles stayed rigid for a minute, then gave in and let his head fall to her shoulder.

"I'm scared," he admitted in a whisper.

Julie kissed his hair and waited for him to speak again.

Miles stared down at the carpet, his eyes seeing dull

brown fibers, his mind remembering a blanket of petals. "It pulls at me, Julie. All the time. It doesn't matter what I'm doing or what I try. It's like I can't win no matter what I do. I don't know why I'm even trying. And, really, I'm not. I haven't used the flute. I'm scared to. But I just keep slipping away, a little deeper each time. And all the while I ache, feeling like if I don't go to find Terris I'll die. It's ridiculous, and I know that, but I can't help it. And I don't know how to stop this. I'm too scared to try anything, so I do nothing. I'm being dragged down to hell an inch at a time instead of all at once." He shut his eyes and sighed, a little raggedly. "And I'm so *tired*. But the worst thing I can do is go to sleep. That much I know."

"I can help you with the sleeping part," Julie said gently. She was stroking his hair. "But first I want to talk to you about something."

Miles lifted his head and looked at her. "What's that?"

Her hand never stopped stroking his hair, but she looked out across the room at nothing in particular, her eyes soft and sad as she said, "Being scared."

Miles stilled. He wasn't sure why, but he had the feeling they were on something of the edge of a precipice here. "Okay," he said at last.

Julie kept her gaze unfocused, still lifted across the room as she continued. "I know that Patty and Katie don't really quite believe you, or that they believe you but keep thinking there's some rational explanation. I expected that from Patty. I'm a little surprised at Katie, but then, when I really think about it, it makes sense. Katie likes ritual, and she likes control. She doesn't like the mystical side of magick—not the true mystery. She believes in a universe she can master, and she deliberately narrows the world to fit that mental image. The idea that some Lord of Dreams could randomly kidnap men and enslave them upsets her. I had hoped it would do so enough for her to challenge it, but—" Julie flattened her lips and shook her head.

Then she turned toward him and looked directly into his eyes.

"I believe you, Miles," she said. "I believe you because I know there are worlds out there we cannot see or understand. I know, because I've seen them myself."

Miles's eyes widened. "You mean you've seen him too? Terris? Or the Lord of Dreams?"

"Not that world, no. But I've seen others. I've seen them all the time since I was little. Not worlds outside of our own as much as worlds within, though I've seen the other kind too. I can talk to animals. Not with my mouth, but it's like I look into their eyes and we're talking to each other. I look into anthills and know what they're doing, why they're moving, and I feel what they feel. It's not feeling like we know it, but there's something there, much more than we think there is. I can see the worlds that layer over our own too. I've seen fairies, and I've seen angels. I've seen the pixies that live in flowers. I've seen all the things that aren't supposed to be true but are. And I've never told any-one else about this before. Not once. Not even Patty."

That didn't surprise Miles. Patty would never un-derstand something like this. Miles couldn't have either as early as a week ago. Now, though—now he under-stood completely.

"That's why you're vegan. Because of the animals. And—the pixies, and things." She nodded, but then he frowned. "Wait, but you raise chickens! And you send them to be slaughtered! And I've seen you prepare beef!"

Julie sighed. "It's the compromise I've had to make. I can't make everyone vegan, much as I would like to sometimes. I can't even make most people vegan. I can't even run my bakery completely vegan. Oh, some people will buy my vegan goods, but not enough to keep us solvent. So I do my best. I keep vegan myself, and I encourage others to follow my example, but I use eggs and cheese and yes, sometimes even meat because it's what brings us money. I try to use only products from good practice. And yes, sometimes I have to kill a chicken to pay the light bill. I do my best to ease their pain, to make it as clean a death as possible. I talk to them the whole time, and I do what I can. That's what I've had to do, Miles, to survive. I used to lie in bed, worried about all the horrible things I knew were happening but I couldn't stop. I used to despair over what I could not fix. I do my best, and I do what I can. I listen to my heart, and I find ways to be compassionate to those other worlds, the worlds of animals and fairies and all the wonders, and when I can't, I apologize, and I mourn. I've found my peace in compromise." She took his hand. "You can too."

She nodded at the silver flute lying on the coffee table. "Don't stall yourself by focusing on what you can't do or what might go wrong. Use what you know. Use what you have. Use your intelligence, Miles. Use your wit. Use your handiness. You're good at puzzles, at fixing things. Use that. Use all of it. And above all"—she reached out and put a hand to his chest, right over his heart—"use this."

Miles tucked his head so he could look down at her hand, so small and slender, so fragile but so warm, so gentle—and all of a sudden his eyes were blurry from unshed tears.

"I don't want to screw up again," he whispered. He held the tears back by sheer force of will, but his voice broke as he added, "I can't take that, not anymore."

"You didn't screw up, Miles," Julie said gently. "You had bad luck."

"I don't have anything," he said, gruffly. "Nothing, Julie. No money, no career, no boyfriend, no confidence—I have nothing but this horrible aching for a man who might want to kill me, who may be turning me over to a man who wants to enslave me."

"You have me," Julie pointed out, "and Patty. And even Katie. Don't listen to the shadows of your heart, Miles, the yearnings. Listen to its beat. Feel its pulse.

Feel the life inside you that connects you to all life. Feel the part of you that no one can hurt, no one can destroy. Feel your soul, Miles, and trust in its wisdom." She brushed a kiss across his cheek. "Come on. Let me help you sleep."

Miles had his doubts about this, but it turned out she knew what she was doing. She laid him on a blanket on the floor, and as he held himself rigid, she whispered, calling to people he could not see, asking them to come watch over him. Miles didn't know if she was calling ghosts or pixies or angels or something else entirely. He didn't ask, and very soon he didn't care. He was just grateful. Because as the invisible visitors circled around him, he could feel them. He couldn't see them, but he could feel their warmth and their protection. He felt the safe space they created for him, and most importantly, he felt the pull of the Lord of Dreams cease. It was temporary, he knew. But it was enough.

He dreamed of tiny little people who held his hands and danced with him in a circle all night long.

When he woke, he was refreshed. He didn't know anything more than when he'd gone to sleep, but he felt collected and recharged, and he felt positive for the first time. He had a plan, too, and he was going to pursue it right after breakfast.

Julie waited for him in the kitchen, and she smiled warmly as he pulled up a stool at the breakfast bar. "Hungry?" she asked, but she was already pulling a carton of eggs out of the refrigerator.

But as she set them down to get a bowl, Miles stared at the eggs with new eyes. He thought of the chicks the eggs could have been. He thought of the horrible living conditions chickens had in factory farms, a fact which he'd known the night before, but this morning somehow seemed more poignant. He thought of the little people who had danced in his dreams, the people Julie had called for him.

He thought of Julie.

When she reached for the eggs, he caught her hand and stopped her. She looked at him, surprised.

"Could I—" He glanced at the eggs again, thought of how good they tasted, but then thought of what it would mean for Julie to make them for him, of the apologies she would have to make. There wasn't any contest.

He cleared his throat. "Can I just have what you're having?"

Julie's face went soft, and she kissed him hard and full on the mouth. When he blinked, she laughed, face flushed with happiness. Then she put the eggs back into the fridge and began pulling out supplies in earnest.

"You won't miss them," she promised, and Miles smiled, his heart full, knowing that she was right. He wouldn't.

Miles rose and crossed the room and started rooting around in the drawer underneath the microwave.

"What are you doing?" Julie asked as she measured out potatoes and onion and tofu.

"Looking for my tools. I'm going to fix your food processor," he said. He paused long enough to accept her kiss, then began to search in earnest.

AFTER BREAKFAST, MILES went to the library and researched silver.

It would have taken him ten minutes on Google, but he still didn't trust himself with computers, so he did it the old-fashioned way—he looked up the information in books. He sat for an hour with a notebook and a pen and a pile of science books and encyclopedias, and when he had all the notes he could take, he headed over to the café, ordered a bottomless cup of coffee, spread his notes out over the table, and tried to make it all make sense. It wasn't an easy task.

Silver, he quickly learned, was an interesting metal full of useful properties, but nothing he learned about it explained Terris, Harry, or the elusive Lord of Dreams. He learned silver was a great conductor of electricity, that it was used in photography because it was the best refractor of light. Silver had antibacterial properties and had been used in wound dressing for a long, long time. It wasn't poisonous, but vapors could make you sick and eventually dead. Electrospinning technology allowed silver to be used in fabrics. The alchemical symbol for silver was once the same as the symbol for the moon. It was stable in water. It was vulnerable to nitric acid and concentrated sulfuric acid. It was an ideal catalyst. It was used in mirrors, cutlery, and jewelry.

And phalluses.

Miles leaned back and tossed his pen onto the table. None of this was helping. He was barking up the wrong tree, clearly, no closer to an answer than he'd been when he began.

"Oh, I don't know about that," a voice said from across the table.

Miles jerked his head up and saw Terris sitting on the other side of his booth. "Oh God. I'm dreaming again."

"You're always dreaming, darling." Terris put his chin in his hand and leaned over the table, surveying the mess of Miles's notes. He was wearing his white coat again, and his long silver hair spilled over his shoulders, shining in the dull light of the café. He extended an elegant finger toward the paper in front of Miles where he'd begun cataloging all the silver things he'd seen since this whole business started. "Here. You want to keep focusing here."

Miles glanced around. There weren't many people in the café in the middle of the afternoon, but there were a few. "Can anyone else see you?"

"That's a good question," Terris observed without looking up from Miles's notes. He reached for a styrofoam cup which looked like it had a vanilla milkshake in it and took an absentminded sip from the straw. He made a face, swallowed, then nodded. "Yes, you're very thorough, aren't you? I'm not sure there's a property of silver that you missed here. You have everything but the Old English translation, I think."

Miles frowned down at his notes. "How in the world would that help anything?"

"You might as well ask how knowing that 'silver is stable in water' will be helpful," Terris said.

Miles threw down his pencil and glared at his companion. "Certainly *you* aren't going to be much of an assistance. You work for *him*, that Lord of Dreams. You're trying to serve me up for his lunch."

Terris clucked his tongue. "He knows so much about silver, but so little about anything else."

"Then tell me." A few people from nearby tables glanced at Miles, but he ignored them. "Tell me what the hell is going on here!"

"Why would you trust me, if you think I'm serving you up for lunch?"

"I don't, but at this point I'll take any information I can get, even lies."

Terris regarded him coolly for several minutes. Miles tried to look defiant, but he knew it was worthless because Terris could read his mind. *That'd be a nice start*, he thought, bitterly, *knowing why he can read my mind. Not that he's going to tell me.*

"Why isn't half as interesting as *how*." Terris sounded amused, like always, but this time there was a funny edge about him. He picked up his milkshake again, took a sip, then passed it over to Miles. "Here. Try it."

Miles gave him a withering look. "You expect me to believe that you're reading my mind with a vanilla milkshake?"

Terris arched an eyebrow and shook the cup enticingly.

Would he try to kill me? Miles wondered, and Terris rolled his eyes. Miles sighed and took a sip.

He gagged.

Terris took the cup back and helped himself again, then looked curiously into the cup. "Do you think vanilla would mask it? I have my doubts, but it could be worth a try." He passed it back over to Miles and tilted his head to the side. "Is that any better?"

Miles, still cringing from his first sip, hesitantly took another. If anything, it was worse than the first time. "It tastes like I'm licking the back of a filmstrip," he said, gagging. "With a hint of vanilla."

Terris shrugged, resigned, and took the cup back. But his eyes were dancing, and he stared hard at Miles, as if waiting for something. Miles fidgeted under the scrutiny, half-afraid to find out what Terris was going to do now. Nothing happened. The only thing that changed was that there was this faint buzzing sensation in his head, probably from stress.

Terris pursed his lips and shook his head. He passed the cup over again. "Just one more sip, but not a big one. Despite your fears, I have no interest in hurting you."

Miles wanted to tell him to fuck off and take his disgusting milkshake with him, but there was something in Terris's expression that made him hesitate. The buzzing grew louder, and he started to feel dizzy. He looked warily at the cup. What the hell was in there?

"What did you tell me it tasted like?" Terris asked, in a question that wasn't a question so much as a prompt. Then his hand strayed to Miles's notes and pointed to a paragraph.

Miles read through them out loud, frowning and pressing his fingers against his temple to ward off the headache that had crept up out of nowhere. "Refractor. Used in photography as silver nitrate, silver bromide, silver iodine—" Miles stopped short. *Like licking a filmstrip.* He looked up at Terris, eyes wide. There was *silver* in this milkshake?

"Sorry, darling, I was pointing to the paragraph where you said that it was a conductor." Except that he hadn't—that wasn't even on that page. Terris kept his stare leveled at Miles. "High concentrations cause dizziness, disorientation, headaches, and unconsciousness." Terris tilted the cup toward Miles. "Just a tiny sip more."

The buzzing was getting louder, and Miles could swear there was a whisper in it now: *drink it, drink it, drink it.* He didn't want to—what Terris just said meant it was poison. But the buzzing urged him on, and before he knew it, he leaned forward and closed his lips around the straw, drawing more of the toxic stuff inside him.

—not too much, not too much. Stop, Miles. Stop drinking now.

Miles did stop, startling so hard that the whole table jolted. He stared at Terris, who regarded him innocently.

Conductor of electricity. What is thought if not electricity across the brain? And under the right circumstances, it can easily be transferred from one brain to another. With the right catalyst.

Miles's eyes went wide, and he fell back against the back of the booth, only remembering to breathe when his vision started to go black.

Terris leaned back too. All his playful, arrogant guise was gone, and he stared at Miles coldly. Blankly. "It won't last very long in your system," he said out loud. "So don't waste time gawking. Go on, darling. Go in and have a peek around."

For a second all Miles could do was quietly panic. He could feel the connection into Terris' mind as if someone had hooked a cable between them, and it was maddening. Everything felt like a hot rush, strange and terrible and loud. He tried to shut his eyes, but it didn't do him any good—it was in his *head.*

And then, slowly, it began to calm, like a wave pulling back. Something gently urged him forward, and he went, hesitant, growing bolder as he went deeper. *This was Terris's mind.* There were no lies here—it was like hearing someone talk about going to a foreign country versus going there yourself. He could see it all. He could *feel* it all. He could feel everything about Terris, all his wants, his needs; his mysteries were all here, open and exposed.

They were terrible.

Terris's mind was full of shadows—*full*, like long planks standing on end, a thousand shields hiding pieces of him from some greater, bigger shadow that lurked around every corner. Miles wound down strange hallways, tiptoeing because he knew something terrible was on the other side, but he knew, too, that whatever it was could not find him here.

So many secrets. There were words that could not be spoken, thoughts which must not be thought, because if they were uttered, the shelters would fall, and it would all be over.

Lonely. It was so lonely here and had been for so long. Only the one had come close to entering within, and what a disaster that had been. *Not my fault. I gave him a choice.* But there was regret there, and sorrow, and fear.

And now there was another—he'd been smarter this time, but it hadn't worked. Why? He'd been so careful! So exact! He'd done it all right, but it hadn't worked. It had to be *him*. But how? The sacrifice and the other hadn't had any contact, so how could it be? How, how, how?

So cold, so cold, so alone...

I am so much better than this!

Seolfor, seolfor, seolfor, seolfor…

The buzzing began again, and Miles felt himself fade back into his own mind. But even before he landed, he started shaking. He stared at Terris, mouth agape, eyes unblinking, tears thickening his throat. He'd seen it all. He knew everything there was to know about Terris. He knew what he had been. He knew how he'd come to the Lord of Dreams, knew how he'd been imprisoned, and he knew how he was trying to get out. He knew how he'd tried to get out before. He shut his eyes. *Oh, Harry.*

"You can say that I am despicable," Terris said calmly. "You can say that I am cruel. I suppose I couldn't argue with you. But, out of curiosity—do you blame me? Would you, put in my place, behave differently?"

Miles would have laughed, but he was afraid he might cry instead. "Yes, I would have behaved differently." Eyes still closed, he shook his head. "But no. I don't blame you."

Terris's hand stole across the table and captured Miles's own. "Will you give yourself to me, Miles, and set me free?"

It was a trap. Even without the silver, he still remembered, and he knew that Terris had set this up, had forced himself into being and followed Miles here, lured him into this conversation and even the drink, exposed himself *all so he could do this*, so that he could move Miles by pity, fear, or, if he were lucky, compulsion to present himself as an offering. *His soul.* And unlike the Lord of Dreams, Miles would not die by pleasure, but by the most exquisite sort of pain as his soul spun out like a ladder, a bridge for Terris to crawl out on, into death, life, or something else. It was impossible to know what exactly would happen, but Terris's departure would take Miles with him, and they would go there together, Terris whole, Miles in ruins. But they would not be in the prison of the Lord of Dreams. That was all that mattered. Because this loneliness, this pain, this agony could not be borne, not anymore. Not for anything.

It wasn't pity or fear that drew Miles, but something far more lethal: fellow feeling.

He let Terris lead him out of the café, his notes clutched awkwardly against his chest. Terris paid his bill with silver coin, and the waitress took it in a dreamy, absent state. Together Miles and Terris went through the trees behind the parking lot, and then they were in the forest, then the castle.

"It's not your castle," Miles said, his voice slurred as he followed Terris down the hall. "It's not really a castle at all. It's inside your mind. It's where you live, all by yourself, and there's no one here. You could go and be with him, but that's worse, and so you're here. You found me because I was vulnerable, and I was a good shot at getting out."

"Yes." Terris eased him onto a silver mattress and looked down at him with real longing. "Will you give me my escape, Miles?"

Drugged by silver, lured by empathy, and lost in the dream, Miles nodded and opened his arms.

There was little foreplay this time, but there was hardly any need. Terris opened Miles and pushed inside him, and Miles lay back and let him in, feeling himself rising away, wondering what it would be like to feel that kind of pain, to be held up so high, to be spun out like an endless thread between two universes, then catapulted into something that he couldn't even comprehend. He opened and arched into his lover, his murderer, and he waited.

Nothing happened.

He was aroused, because he always was with Terris—but he couldn't give himself to him because he could not come. He couldn't exit his body, couldn't ride with him out of his hell, couldn't give Terris his release. Even though he gave himself freely, it wasn't working. No matter how much he let go, something in him held back. No matter how Terris plunged inside him, no matter how he pleaded or coaxed, Miles could not give him his release.

Terris finally collapsed forward onto Miles's body, clutched the silver bedding in his fists, and screamed.

"*Why?*" he cried, half raging, half weeping. "What have I done wrong?" He swore passionately in a language Miles couldn't understand. "I can feel you giving yourself, but it won't work. It's even worse than it was with the other one." He pounded the bed with his fists, shouted again, then withdrew from Miles and rolled away. "Go," he said gruffly. "Just leave me."

Miles stared at him. He felt sick, and he felt confused. He hated Terris, and he ached for him too. He wanted to run, weeping with relief at what he had just escaped, and he wanted to take Terris in his arms and hold him.

Terris snorted. "Don't. Just leave."

Miles turned his head toward Terris and tried to glare, but the weight of his knowledge took the bitter edge from him. "You expect me to know what I know about you and just *leave you?*"

"Oh, if you want to save me, feel free."

But of course, Miles did not know how to save him. He shut his eyes.

"Take heart," Terris said, still mocking. "You'll remember my suffering for the rest of your life, but your life will be but a flutter of a heartbeat of my existence. It will be over for you very soon."

Miles felt sick. "Let me help you, please! I want—"

Terris leapt on him. He had his tongue down Miles's throat, thrusting against him, fucking him roughly without entering him, but Miles only held still and bore it until Terris pulled back again.

"Then *give yourself to me.*" Terris licked his throat. "Just once. *Once,* Miles, and I'm gone. The energy you give during your orgasm is enough to take me away. But you must give yourself to *me.* Not to him. To *me.*"

Miles tried. But once again, it didn't work.

Terris shrieked, a sound more full of pain and rage and helplessness than anything Miles had ever heard, a sound more awful than any look he had seen on Harry's face. He felt a hard slap against his cheek, and then he fell down to earth, down to the patch of weeds outside the café, where Terris left him.

He sat there for a long time, sobbing quietly. Then he rose, gathered up his notes, and drove away. But he didn't go back to the pawn shop or the trailer.

He called Julie, and at her urging, they went to Katie's.

"HE IS A fairy," Miles began.

Katie looked up from her notebook, pen poised. "I assume you aren't making some clever statement on his sexuality. You mean that he is fey? Faerie, with the 'e' and the 'ie' present? Drag-you-under-the-hill faerie, not sprinkle-pixie-dust fairy?"

Her tone was sharp and thick with disbelief, but Miles took comfort in Julie's presence. She sat between them, looking wide-eyed at Miles. *She* believed him.

Miles nodded and drew the blanket closer to his chin as he tucked his feet farther back into the easy chair where Katie had stationed him in front of her fireplace. *Faerie.* Funny how the word tasted different when he changed the spelling in his head.

"He was a musician in the court of a high-ranking faerie, but he was bored, and he thought—" Miles paused, feeling the frightening echo of the words which had been both Terris's and his own. "He thought, *I am so much better than this*. He tried his hand at magic. Except from what I could see it looked more like science. Like alchemy. Whatever it was, it didn't go terribly well, and he got in big trouble. He was banished from the court. In a moment of rage and vulnerability, he gave himself to the Lord of Dreams, who is one of the Old Ones of the faeries. Had he been human, he would have been consumed, like Harry told me he should have been. But he was faerie, so he was simply abused, and then when the Lord grew bored, he was imprisoned." Miles shuddered, remembering the feelings he'd brushed against inside Terris's head. "It's cold where he is. Really, really cold, and very painful. And he's been there a long, long, time."

Katie still looked dubious, but Julie leaned forward, resting her elbows on her knees. "What does he want with you?"

"He wants a way out," Miles said. "Because I have a human soul, he can use that somehow—something between a slingshot and a ladder, as best I can understand."

Julie frowned. "But that sounds like it would kill you."

"Oh, yeah." Miles leaned his head against the side of the chair and stared into the fire. "I think it would have been pretty painful too. But he can't do it. I don't know that he's given up trying with me, but there seems to be some block against his being able to use me that way. And I don't think it has anything to do with the Lord of Dreams. I think it has something to do with Harry."

"Harry?" Julie echoed.

"That's the beast," Katie said, grumbling. "The beast who, if he finds Miles, will rape him out of desperate madness. Nevertheless, Miles happily put on a sex show for him." Katie put down her notebook and covered her cheeks with her hands as she shook her head. "None of this makes any logical sense."

"Logic isn't the important part here," Julie argued, then turned to Miles. "This is bad. You can't let him do this to you."

Katie nodded, a little weary. "I'll put some wards up around you, Miles. But Julie's right. You should let this go."

"I *can't*," Miles said with some heat. "Don't you understand? I *saw*. I saw and I *felt*. You can't imagine what it feels like to feel what I found there in his head. I can't forget this. Not ever." His hands clenched around the frayed edges of the blanket, and he shook his head. "I have to do something. I have to find a way to help him. To help both of them."

"Miles." Julie reached out and put a hand on his leg. "Miles, he is fey. That, by definition, means he is capable of deceit you can't even process, even when it's staring you in the face. Nothing about them is human. Do you understand? *Nothing*. They look like us, but they aren't like us inside. They feel about as much affection for humans as we feel for cockroaches. He wouldn't let you see inside his head if he weren't sure it was to his advantage. This is part of his plan, don't you see?"

Miles brushed her hand away. "I know that already, and it doesn't matter. You didn't see it, Julie. I don't know, maybe if I saw it every day for a week on the evening news I could move on, but you know what? I don't want to. It's like you—" He paused, realizing that Katie was still there, and censored himself. "I can feel what he feels, Julie. I have empathy for him. You guys are always on me to be less selfish, to stop going on about myself and my due. Well, you've got your wish. All I want right now is to help the both of them. I can't think of anything else. I guess I still want to help them for me, because it's the pain in *my* heart that's driving me, but I'm more devoted to this than any bad relationship or job I've ever had."

He rested his head in his hand and stared at the fire. "I saw Harry, too, inside his head. I saw how Terris tried to do the same thing with him that he did with me. He's even worse off, Katie, because Harry does have a soul. That's what's driving him insane. He's caught between two faeries, unwilling to yield to both, but unable to escape and unable to die."

"And how are you going to help?" Katie demanded. "What are you going to do that doesn't trap you the same way, or make things even worse?"

"I don't know," Miles confessed.

"That's why we came to you," Julie said, turning to Katie. "You have studied magick for so much longer than I have. Surely you must know *something* about faeries."

"I know about mythology," Katie snapped. "I know about metaphor and philosophy. I don't know anything about faeries who are *real*."

Julie's shoulders slumped. "Then you can't help him."

Miles rubbed at his face. "I'll just have to do it myself, then."

Katie glared at him. "You don't have any training in this, any at all. You don't even know the *theory* of magick. And yet you're just going to barge in?"

"Yes," Miles snapped. "I don't know what I'm doing, no. But I'm going to figure it out. You can help me, ignore me, or get in my way, but I'm going to do this no matter what."

Katie glared at him a moment, then looked at Julie for support. But Julie still looked disappointed, and eventually Katie threw up her hands and sank back on her chair.

"Tell me, wonderboy," Katie asked, "how does your silver flute fit into this? Have you tried to use it yet?"

"I think it was Terris's," Miles said. "Terris wouldn't talk about it, and I could feel him blocking it inside his head. And one of them said it was the enemy of the Lord of Dreams. I think it was Harry, but it's starting to all blend together in my head. It makes sense, though, if it's Terris's. And there's something with silver. Something *huge* with silver. That's what he used to read my mind, and how he got me to read his. And if the silver flute is the enemy of the Lord of Dreams, that means either silver or music is his vulnerability."

"Whoa, whoa, whoa," Katie said. "Are you listening to yourself? You're nothing but speculation! How are you going to test these theories? By dying stupidly?"

"I don't have that as my plan, no," Miles shot back. "I plan to study, and I plan to think." He bit his lip. "I do plan to try the flute. Soon, I think."

"I don't know that that's such a good idea, given what you've told me about this Terris," Katie said. "What if it gets you into more trouble?"

"Then I'll do my best to get out of it," Miles said. He looked at her patiently. "Is there any practical advice—outside of 'don't do this, it's crazy'—that you would care to give me about fey, or magic, or magick with a k, or even musical instruments?" He looked at Julie, but she only smiled with quiet encouragement. Miles turned back to Katie and waited.

Katie looked at him for a long time. Then she swore under her breath and passed him the notebook and pen as she rose and headed to the kitchen.

Miles's shoulders slumped. "So that's a no?"

"No," Katie said. "That's a 'sit tight while I put on

some tea, and work out your hand cramps, because you are going to take notes like you should have taken them in college.'"

Miles smiled in relief. "I took pretty good notes in college."

"Multiply that by whatever value you put on your life, and you ought to be about where you should be."

"What are you going to tell him about?" Julie asked.

"Folklore. Everything and anything I know about folklore and myth and all the things that I say I believe in but actually don't. Or didn't, until now."

Julie smiled. "I can help with that too."

"Good," Katie said gruffly.

Miles sobered. "Thank you." He took Julie's hand. "Both of you."

"I hope you still feel that way once you start playing that flute." Katie disappeared into the kitchen.

CHAPTER EIGHT

Behind me is loss. Behind me is pain.
Behind me nothing but sorrow can reign.
Do not let me look. Do not let me see.
No more of my life: only pleasure, with thee.

WHEN MILES FINALLY left Katie's house, his head was spinning. His arms ached too. He had a huge box of spell casting supplies as well as a three-ring binder full of notes, some he'd taken, and some Katie had recopied for him from her own files. Julie had promised to give him more materials once they were back at the trailer too.

Julie had stayed behind to discuss a few things with Katie, which left Miles heading home on his own. He was a little uneasy about this, expecting to be snatched out of this world at any time, but Julie had given him a small charm and told him not to worry. Unlike anything of Katie's, Julie's felt warm, and he thought maybe this one might actually work. Still, he took the long way home, away from the woods. At least this time, he got to use the car; Katie had promised to give Julie a ride back when they were finished.

But Miles didn't head home right away. He meandered around town, just cruising, letting his mind wander. His mind kept drifting to Harry and to Terris, to the faerie world where they were imprisoned, possibly forever. Miles thought about what Terris had said about his suffering only lasting the short expanse of his lifetime, then thought of Harry, imprisoned so many lifetimes he had run completely mad. It all weighed on him, so huge, so impossible. He wished he could cast the spell tonight, but now more than ever, he knew he needed to prepare, to study up and to plan. And sleep. Julie had promised to protect his sleep again, but all Miles could think of was that Harry had no one to do that for him. And Terris was in that cold, lonely place inside his mind….

Miles's misery overwhelmed him, and the next thing he knew, he was turning into the bar at the end of Third Street.

It was a small, dingy sort of place, the very antithesis of the kind of bar he'd gone to in Atlanta. There were no sleek chrome lines, no flashing lights or pulsing beats, and no beautiful men decorating bar stools. There was just tinny country music, dilapidated tables and chairs and equally run-down men and women. In short, the bar was as sad as the rest of Summer Hill.

Miles knew about a third of the people there. Most he knew from high school, some from seeing them around town since his return, but none of them were what he would call friends. So he sat in an empty, isolated space at the end of the bar and surveyed the landscape, letting it feed his depression. He ordered a beer on tap. It was watery and acrid, but it suited his mood. He drank the first beer in silence, then settled into the second. It went down a little better.

The third, actually, wasn't bad at all.

In the bottom of the fourth glass, Miles found an almost Zen-like comfort. The music and the ambience that had so annoyed him became a balm as well, and when a grizzled old man sat down next to him, Miles spoke freely to him, telling him about getting fired and losing his boyfriend and then about the Lord of Dreams and Harry and Terris. Suddenly he was very eager to share his tales of woe.

"I would do it," he told the old man, his words slurring. "I would let him kill me and ride me to the other dimmensh—dimmensh"—Miles hiccoughed and waved a hand in irritation—"place. I would. But I can't stop thinking of Harry. I love Harry, I think." He swayed on his stool and looked intently at his listener. "I'd let him fuck me too. Even though his cock is so big. I'd let him. I *would*."

The old man gave Miles an odd look, slipped off the stool, and went around to the other side of the hostess stand, well away from Miles.

Miles toasted his new friend with an empty glass, murmured something incoherent, then set the glass back down. He wanted another beer, but first he needed to piss.

Jesus, did he need to piss.

"I'll play the flute tomorrow," Miles promised himself out loud while he stumbled down the dimly lit hallway toward the toilets. "I'll play it, and I'll figure it out. I'll save them. And then… and then…." He stopped and stared at a velvet Elvis on the wall beside him. What would he do after? He'd free Terris, free Harry, and then… then what would happen to him? Would Harry come back? Would Miles stay with him?

Would he come back to this world, alone? Again?

"No," Miles whispered to Elvis. "Anything but that."

His eyes were blurry as he made his way to the bathroom, and he stumbled inside, heading for a stall instead of a urinal. He needed a wall to lean on while he pissed, he was pretty sure. And he did piss—he pissed a royal fucking river. When he was done, he tucked himself back in his pants, his fingers numb, which made him laugh. Then, suddenly, he wanted to cry. He hurried back out of the stall before he could.

Warren was there.

For a moment, they stood and stared at one another, surprised. For a moment neither of them moved. Warren looked like a fatter, taller, and scruffier version of what Miles supposed he must look like: his eyes were bloodshot, his clothes were untidy, and his fly was clumsily done. There was a haunted look about his eyes that hinted that he'd been trying to drown his misery but hadn't quite managed it. He'd pushed it aside, perhaps, but it was there, waiting and ready to push him back under again at any second. He looked defeated, and weary, and very, very pathetic.

In that moment, Miles felt an odd affinity for his old enemy.

But then the moment passed, and they moved into their old roles like they were stepping into a familiar dance. Warren murmured a slur beneath his breath, and Miles cowered, backing up into the stall, which of course was a very big mistake. Because this was one of those moments where Warren was not going to belittle him and make him parrot self-loathing statements. This was when Warren used Miles to vent his own failure, to deal with his own inadequacies. This was where Warren bought himself a few moments of ease by giving some of his pain to Miles. In Miles's drunken state, the act seemed almost logical, and he yielded as Warren gripped his shoulder and thrust him farther inside, then pushed him down toward the toilet bowl, seat still dripping with Miles's bad aim. And, sadly, the bowl was not flushed. Even so, Miles still did not fight.

This was what he was. This was how pathetic his life had become, how, really, it had always been. Terris was right. Atlanta, his success, all of it had just been a dream. This was his reality.

His horrible, depressing reality.

But before Warren even had him turned around,

Miles felt his attacker stiffen, then heard him cry out softly. Miles turned his head to see what had caught Warren's attention, and then he froze too.

A man was hovering over the toilet. A silver, transparent man.

It wasn't Terris, and not Harry, and somehow, Miles knew this was not the Lord of Dreams. This, actually, was the man that Miles had dreamt had sat at the foot of his bed when this had all started. This was the man he'd seen at the edge of the forest. This was the man who had appeared in Katie's circle.

How many men *were* there after him?

And—wait, Warren could see him too?

He glanced back over his shoulder and saw that Warren had gone very pale. He was staring at the ghost man, shaking his head. Miles was entirely forgotten.

The ghost man drifted forward, and Miles watched in drunken wonder as the beautiful, transparent face twisted into a smile.

"*Boo,*" it said.

Warren screamed, stumbled out of the stall, and ran out of the bathroom.

Miles turned back to the ghost, wondering why he wasn't afraid, wondering what this was all about, wondering what he was supposed to do now. The ghost, as if sensing his questions, turned to him.

"*Play the flute,*" he said.

"Who are you?" Miles whispered.

The ghost didn't answer, just regarded Miles for a

few minutes. Then he reached up and touched Miles's cheek with cold, ghostly fingers. He smiled sadly.

"You cannot live in dreams, Miles. But remember that reality is what you make of it, and that your disappointment is not your truth."

Miles frowned, but before he could ask the ghost what the hell that meant, the man faded again, and Miles was left alone, drunk, lonely, and confused, staring at the faded graffiti on the wall.

THREE DAYS AFTER he saw the ghost man in the bathroom, Miles played the flute. And at Katie and Julie's suggestion, he played it inside a circle.

It was a circle he'd cast himself, which was something he never thought he'd do. Despite all the hoodoo he'd witnessed lately, he still felt silly calling North and South and East and West and sprinkling salt, and he had a feeling the things he'd gathered for his altar were pretty paltry. But he did take the spell seriously—seriously enough to cast it in the attic storeroom above the shop and at a time when no one was around. He was naked again, too, and he'd taken a makeshift bath in a basin just a few feet away. *Contaminants*, Katie had said. Who knew what and how little of it would mess up a spell like this? She'd told him to go into the circle with nothing but himself to the best of his ability, and that's what he had done.

Julie had told him to ask for the Mother Moon to

guide him, to help him, and to protect him. Miles had tried, but not much had happened. He was too nervous to try again. Also, he was so cold he couldn't think of anything else. It was drafty in the attic.

When he finished casting, he surveyed the scene, trying to decide if he could really feel the circle and the four elements or if this was just his mind playing tricks on him. Then he decided it didn't matter and picked up the flute. He turned it over a few times in his hand, took a deep breath, and drew it to his lips.

This he definitely could feel.

He kept his tone clear and simple, sending humility and as many good feelings as he could through the instrument. Julie had stressed that this was the most crucial point of all, especially the humility.

"Anything that old has a life of its own, and a consciousness," she'd said. "It is probably faint, but it's there, and it will be watching you closely. Think of it like approaching a dog or a horse. It will know if you're nervous or if you're planning evil intent. If you come at the flute in a pure manner, you'll know pretty fast if it harbors negative energy or not. If you're pure and it isn't, it will slap you back. Anything else it will try to use. So be careful."

Miles was careful. He played the scale up and down for fifteen minutes or so, slowly, patiently, all the while thinking, *I am humble. I come with pure intent. I come for the purpose of good and light and healing. I am humble. I come with pure intent.* Over and over and over, the scale and the mental chant a litany, and it didn't take long for him to truly mean it. Without quite meaning to, he also began to think of Harry and of Terris, of their plights as he had heard and seen and understood, and he took a chance and revealed, too, his empathy.

The flute didn't do much, but it felt warm and gentle in his hands. Julie hadn't said exactly what it would do if it were an instrument of good—the pun was killing him—but she had warned him that it could trick him no matter what. So he kept playing his scale, shutting his eyes and thinking of Terris's pain and how much it made him, Miles, ache, and how unfair he felt all this was to Harry. He played the scale and felt his feelings, over and over and over and over and over. When he grew tired and dizzy from so much playing, he put the instrument down and opened his eyes.

The entire space inside the circle with him had filled up with tiny, glistening silver flowers. They had grown up out of the floorboards of the storeroom.

Miles put the flute down carefully. Neither Julie or Katie had said *anything* about this.

He touched one of the petals tentatively. They felt like flower petals, but he was pretty sure they were real silver. He shook his head in amazement. How had this happened? He gnawed on his bottom lip. Was it a good sign? Flowers certainly didn't seem bad, per se. He touched the stem of one of them carefully, then plucked it. It came easily into his hand.

Okay, then.

Miles ran his hands over the flowers a few more times, trying to decide what to do next. More scales? A song? He had no idea. Katie had said he'd need to go on instinct here, but to stay humble. He nodded. Okay. That's what he'd do.

He picked up the flute again, but this time he didn't raise it to his lips right away. He held it, closed his eyes and whispered, "Show me what I should ask you to see."

Then, hands shaking, trying to project love and peace and humility, he brought the flute back up. As it settled into place against his lip, he felt a strange tingle run through his body; he took a breath, and before he could let it out, the tingling rushed again.

Miles slipped into a trance, and he began to play.

He didn't know the song he played. It wasn't even tonal, not really, and it was far more technical than he had ever played in high school. The flute, he realized dimly, was playing him. It made him nervous, but at this point there was no backing out, so he remembered what Katie said, clung to love and light and humility, and held on for the ride.

When the song stopped, he opened his eyes.

The storeroom was gone. His salted circle ring was glowing silver on top of some matted grass, and Miles—and all his silver flowers—sat in its center. He was in a forest now, not the forest outside the trailer park, but in a place Miles had never been before. As he studied his surroundings a little more carefully, he was pretty sure this was a *world* he'd never been before.

The trees were taller than any he had ever seen, and they were oddly shaped: they looked like trees drawn in storybooks, with fat trunks and willowy branches that arranged themselves into picturesque forms and pleasing shapes. In short, they were the sorts of trees that did not grow on their own in the wild but were cultivated. Except nobody ever cultivated a forest; it was too big. This was a forest designed by Disney. It was beautiful. It was perfect.

It was, Miles realized, the sort of forest a faerie would design.

He drew his knees up against his chest and looked around. The leaves were all different colors, hovering around what could be considered normal greens and yellows, but they were just a little too much of whatever color they happened to be. A few of the trees had given it up altogether and boasted leaves which were almost blue. The bark of the trees was either rich and brown, or pale, lovely gray. When it suited the leaves above them, the bark was peppered with green moss. The plants below the trees were flowers, growing through the patches of sun, which aimed themselves just right. The paths were not strewn with sticks but were all evenly packed lines of dirt, accented prettily with smooth round stones. The place where Miles sat was a small clearing, full of flowers and grasses that did not reach too high. All stumps were nicely arranged and ready-worn for sitting.

The only thing out of place was a shadow beneath one of the trees, and as Miles stared at it, he realized that this was not a shadow, but a man. Then the man stepped forward, and Miles saw that it was a beast.

It was Harry.

One glance told Miles that the man he had met in the dungeon was long gone, as Harry had warned him. The beast that crept cautiously out of the shadows lumbered, sniffing the air. He eyed Miles and his circle warily, and when he saw the ring of flowers, he snorted and stamped at the ground.

"*Nā seolfor,*" the beast growled.

Miles had climbed to his feet at the first sight of Harry, but he looked down now at the tiny metallic blooms beneath his feet. That word again. Damn it, he had to figure it out! He rubbed his cheek, frowning at the ground. Was it something in the magic? The flute?

"What is *seolfor*?" Miles asked Harry, not expecting an answer, but unable to think of any other place to start.

Harry snorted again and stamped at the circle. "*Seolfor.*"

Miles indicated the circle with his finger. "This? The circle?" He plucked a flower and held it up.

Harry roared and stepped back. "*Seolfor!*"

Miles dropped the flower. "Silver. That's what that word is, isn't it? Silver." The conversation with Terris at the café came back, and he almost laughed. "God! He told me, didn't he! He said I had everything but the Old

English translation. And that's what that word is. *Seolfor* is silver."

"*Nā seolfor!*" Harry shouted.

"Do you speak English?" Miles asked. "Modern English?" He racked his brain for the annals of his Brit Lit series, for the memorized passages which had been so useless right up until now. "'Whan that Aprill, with his shoures soote, the droghte of March hath perced to the roote....' Shit, no, Chaucer is *Middle* English, not Old."

He shut his eyes and rubbed at his temple, trying to retrieve another passage. Then he looked up at Harry again.

"'*Hwæt! We Gardena in geardagum, þeodcyninga, þrym ge-frunon, hu ða æpelingas, ellen fremedon.*' At least I think that's the opening to *Beowulf*." He grimaced. "Of course, I don't remember what I just said, and I can't imagine—"

But Harry was looking at him intently. "*Scóp?*"

Miles blinked, then clapped and laughed. "Harry! Harry, you're Old English! Or, rather, you speak it. But you're from England! You *are* from this world!"

Harry lumbered forward, pointing angrily to the ring of silver. "*Náhtfremmend!*"

Whatever that word was, it wasn't a good one. Miles held out his hands. "Please—I don't understand. Please, Harry—it's me, Miles. I don't speak Old English, I only quote epic poems a professor made me memorize. Please—you spoke to me before. I know you're there. Please, Harry!"

But Harry wasn't there. Just the beast, pawing angrily at the ground.

Miles wanted to scream. He hated the perfect forest, hated the Lord of Dreams and Terris, hated all of it for wrapping him up inside and not letting him go. Harry was his only real friend in this. Harry was the one he truly felt for. Terris was just another manipulator, however much Miles empathized with him. But it killed Miles to see the kind, articulate man he'd known in the dungeon reduced to this, and for he himself to be so helpless to aid him.

He picked up the flute and shut his eyes, and he thought desperately at it. *Please. Please, help me, even just to talk to him.* He put the flute to his lips, drew a breath, and began to play.

Harry screamed and stumbled backward toward the trees.

"No!" Miles dropped the flute and reached for him. "No, wait!"

But Harry just kept screaming and turned to run.

"*No!*" Miles cried and took a step forward.

There was a crackle and a snap. Miles shut his eyes against a bright light, then gasped as he felt something wrap around him like lightning, close and smothering. Then it was gone, and he could breathe, and he opened his eyes.

He stood in a patch of sunlight, wearing a plain, lightweight suit of silver cloth. He was also standing outside the circle.

The circle and the flute were gone.

Harry stopped, looked at Miles, and his eyes changed, glowing with a silver heat.

"*Gástlufu,*" he whispered and started lumbering toward Miles. His hands were outstretched, his claws clicking against one another. His eyes darkened further. "*Gástlufu!*"

Miles cried out, turned around, and ran.

CHAPTER NINE

THE PERFECT FAERIE forest made a strange background as Miles fled from Harry. Instead of stepping on sticks and rotted stumps, he vaulted over artfully arranged round stones and stomped on mushrooms that could have housed the caterpillar in Wonderland. He would have done better in a normal forest, because there he could have leapt over the sorts of things a cloven-hoof man would have to take the time to climb. As it was, the path was practically a road, and Harry and his goat-hooves were quickly gaining.

"*Gástlufu,*" Harry cried over and over. "*Gástlufu! Gástlufu!*"

Miles whimpered and tried to lose Harry by weaving between trees. Harry was so close now that he was starting to swipe at Miles, and twice Miles felt the brush of his claws. *Maybe that was another lie, that Harry would rape me. Maybe Terris lied. Maybe he lied to Harry too. Maybe—*

"*Gástlufu!*" A claw caught the fabric of Miles's shirt. It fell away, but the motion made Miles stumble, and the next thing he knew, he was pitching face-first into the grass, Harry's weight pressing on top of him.

Harry roared, pinned Miles's shoulders to the ground, and began to grunt and thrust against his backside.

Miles gagged as the rotten-animal stink of Harry smothered him, then coughed and gasped as the force of Harry's exertions pushed his mouth and nose into the grass. "No, Harry," he rasped, trying to turn his head and failing. "*Harry!*" His fingers curled into the dirt and stones until they bled, his mind and body going into shock as Harry tore roughly at his clothes, trying to bare him.

He was going to do it. Terris hadn't lied, and Harry had been right. There was no man in there, just a beast, and it was going to rape him, naive, hopeful fool that he was. He felt the fabric of his clothes tear, then felt the brush of Harry's furry arm against his bare ass. Choking back a sob, Miles gritted his teeth and locked his body, trying to brace as Harry grabbed his legs and wrenched them apart.

And then Harry was gone, howling and crying out. "*Seolfor! Náhtfremmend!*"

Miles reeled for a second, stunned by the realization that he was not, in fact, being rent apart, then climbed to his feet with a sob of relief. He clutched his clothes around him as best he could, daring to glance over his shoulder as he began to run again. Then what he had seen registered, and he stopped.

Harry was still howling, standing in the middle of the path and looking down at his hands, which were full of blood. Miles reached around to his back in panic, but his flesh was whole. This was Harry's own blood.

What was even stranger was that Harry's claws were gone. The beast was howling in pain, staring down at his very bloody, very human hands.

Empathy ripped through Miles, and before he knew what he was doing, he had started forward.

Harry howled and staggered back toward a thicket of daisies.

The light shifted, and for a moment the forest looked ominous and black. A sharp summer wind drifted past Miles's nose, full of fragrance and sun and heavy stupor. It made Miles want to giggle and laugh, to strip off his clothes and lie down in the road, waiting for a pleasure he knew would come.

Miles's nostrils flared, and he covered his face with his ragged sleeve. "Terris." He loped back into the cover of some bushes, holding up his pants with his other hand as he went. As he pulled the leaves around his head, he saw a figure form in the middle of the path in the place where Harry had been standing. But it was not Terris. It was a man, yes, but he was taller, and darker, and even from behind, Miles could tell that he was ten times more handsome than Terris could ever hope to be.

Miles was in the presence of the Lord of Dreams.

The Lord turned, and on a sliver of instinct, Miles shut his eyes tight. He could feel the Lord of Dreams staring at him, trying to find him, trying to draw him out. It was like being burned, and he knew that if he opened his eyes or so much as let down his mental guard he would be lost. He shut his eyes tighter and tried to think of the flute. *Come back. Come back, and take me out of here.*

The flute didn't come. But the Lord didn't see Miles, either, and after a few minutes, he turned away again.

Miles let out a silent, ragged sigh of relief. Then his world rocked again when he heard the faerie speak.

"What is this racket, Beast?"

The words seemed to wrap around Miles, sliding inside his head as well as filtering through his ears. He clutched at the branches of the brush in which he hid, forcing his eyes to stay closed. It was difficult even to breathe in the presence of the Lord of Dreams. Miles's body felt hot and tight, and he realized it was because despite the fact that he was cold with terror, he was also acutely aroused. He was aware of his own scent, and that of Harry, and more than anything he was aware of the Lord. Miles knew if he could but gaze upon the Lord of Dreams, he would never want for anything but him again. He would be frozen by his own desire, and he would sit here and die from it, like an addict, so enraptured by pleasure that he forgot that he was even alive. That was how you died in the pleasure of the Lord of Dreams. Empty, senseless pleasure.

And in a vision, he could see all the victims of the Lord, human and otherwise, hollow husks of men dotted over the landscape of beauty, withering and dying in their own lust.

All but Terris. All but Harry.

Why?

Harry was still crying. *"My hands, my hands! The evil-doer is within my beloved, and he has ruined my hands!"*

Miles gasped and gritted his teeth against a wave of nausea. He heard Harry's reply in grunts and howls, but he also heard the words inside his head. *My enchantment.* But why hadn't it worked before?

The image of Harry's bloody hands flashed into Miles's mind.

Blood? Had the blood done it? Had the blood turned his claws to hands and translated his words?

The Lord of Dreams clucked his tongue. "Poor mad beast. You're even worse than usual today. And look, you have indeed done something to your hands. Extraordinary!" There was another howl, and then a whimper. "No," the Lord of Dreams scolded. "No fussing. You will allow me to inspect them, or it will go badly for you."

Harry howled again, then roared. The cry tore through Miles, and he had to bite his lip to keep from calling back.

The Lord of Dreams sighed. "You could make this easier on both of us and surrender your will to me."

"*Beloved!*" Harry cried. And as the word came out alone, Miles recognized it as the one he'd been calling out so much before. *Gástlufu.*

Beloved.

"Yes, yes, I know," the Lord of Dreams said dryly. "You will only surrender to your beloved. I don't—" He stopped, then hissed and swore.

Harry cried out again. "*Silver!*"

"Yes," the Lord said icily. "So you said, and so I should have believed. I take it our mutual friend has been up to mischief again? Perhaps I should check in on him and tell him what I think of hiding bits of silver cloth beneath your fingernails? Odd, though, I must say. I'd expect him to put a ring around your cock, because that's his kind of cruelty." There was a pause, and when the faerie spoke again, his voice was thoughtful. "But no. Dear Terris sleeps on. This is not his doing. How very interesting, Beast. Someone *else* is here. Someone, despite the illogic of the statement, whom I cannot see."

"*Beloved,*" Harry wailed.

"Perhaps I should look a bit more closely," the Lord of Dreams said.

The world around Miles began to tighten and

shrink, and his erection, already great, grew so painful he had to bite his hand to keep from crying out. The pressure of the Lord of Dreams pushed so hard around him that he knew if it kept up he would either give in, or he would die. He choked, he shuddered, and as he felt the vessels inside his brain begin to swell, he sent out a fleeting, whispered prayer.

"Help!"

And like a balloon expanding, he felt a force field rise around him. When it passed his head, he dared to open his eyes at last and saw that he was sitting hunched inside a transparent silver sphere. The silver flute was in his hand.

Push, it said.

Miles did.

He pushed with his mind and with his heart, and between that and the force of the flute, they kept the faerie's spell at bay. Miles's heart pounded, and he thought he would be sick, but he was not enslaved by pleasure, and he was not dead. Shaking, he lifted his head and dared a look at the clearing. He could see the back of the Lord of Dreams, and he could see Harry. The Lord looked like a silver shadow-shape to Miles, obscured, he assumed, by the flute's spell. Harry looked like a beacon of light.

At last, the pressure stopped. The silver orb faded, and Miles quickly averted his eyes.

"How very odd," the Lord of Dreams said. He sounded torn between concern and amusement. Miles heard him take several steps, his silken clothes whisper-ing against each other as he walked. "Beast, something is quite wrong here. No more running around, do you understand? Back to your little cave. I want you to stay there until I call you again. I don't want you out in any of the worlds until I sort out what's going on."

"*Beloved!*" Harry cried.

"No more whining," the faerie said sharply. "I'll make more than your hands bleed if you push me, Beast. I'm not in the mood. I must go and deal with whoever this is causing me trouble in my own world. I only hope it's a wizard of some sort, and not another fey. I'd rather be amused than annoyed." He clapped his hands. "Go on with you!"

Harry howled again and lumbered off into the woods.

The Lord of Dreams sighed. "And now for you, whoever you are. I can feel you, so don't think you're cleverer than you are. I can't find you yet, but I will. And you will be sorry, sorrier than you could ever hope to be."

Even without looking, Miles could feel the faerie's departure.

Despite this, he remained huddled in the bushes until he had the strength to stand again. Then with a trembling hand, he raised the flute to his lips.

Take me to Terris, he whispered.

He played a few notes, and he was gone.

THE CRYSTAL DOORS were closed when Miles appeared before them. He knocked, but nothing happened. He tried to open them, but they would not yield.

Miles hitched up his waistband and set out to walk the perimeter. The flute had vanished again, but that didn't worry him any longer. Clearly it would come when he called it—well, if it wanted to come. Anyway, he was in Terris's world now. Neither Harry nor the Lord of Dreams could come here.

It was an echo of the Lord of Dream's house, yes, but Terris had laced it with silver, Miles realized as he searched the exterior of the castle for a way to enter. The Lord of Dreams could not touch silver. Neither could Harry. Except maybe Harry could—it was the beast that could not handle it. And it had transformed him. But it had hurt him.

Miles pushed at a window, swore, then stormed on to find another one.

Terris was under the control of the faerie, but he was separate too. Harry was under the control of the faerie, but the Lord of Dreams did not have his will. That belonged to his beloved, which was what he kept calling Miles. Though the Lord thought that was Terris. But Miles didn't have any power over Harry, not that he understood. If Harry caught Miles, he would indeed rape him. But if Miles were wearing silver, the pain of the silver would make Harry stop.

This was all so confusing.

The next three windows were sealed tight, and the door that led to the silver lakeshore was locked too.

"Terris!" Miles shouted. "Terris, damn you, let me in! I need to talk to you!" But Terris didn't answer.

Miles made his way all around the castle, trying every entrance that he could. Nothing worked. He pounded on the front door again, shouted, and then, hands hurting and heart heavy, he sank against it.

He wondered if maybe he should go back. He wondered if Katie wasn't right, if he shouldn't just give this up. He'd seen the Lord of Dreams, and he'd felt firsthand how unfair the fight was. She was right. He could never stand up to these forces. No one could. Yes, he ached for Harry, even after nearly being raped by him. Terris, he couldn't make up his mind about, but Harry had stolen his heart. And yet, all he was doing was failing him.

Maybe he should just quit.

The flute appeared in his hand, and without directly giving it a command or making a wish, he blew a soft, mournful note.

The castle faded away, and he was back in his room at Patty and Julie's trailer. Miles sighed, heavyhearted, and started for the bed so he could collapse on it.

Then he got a better look at the room and went very still.

It was his room, yes, but it was very strange. It was all dull gray, and it was frozen, like a picture. He wasn't sure how he could tell at first, because nothing in the room was really mobile, but then he tried to pull a tissue out of the box on the edge of the desk. It wouldn't come out, and he got the whole box, frozen as if it were a cardboard cutout. It weighed nothing, and when he dropped it, it fell sideways onto the desk, unmoved. As he watched, it turned to dust.

He wasn't, he realized, actually here. Nothing in the room was real.

But some things were. Some things glittered, and it only took a moment for him to realize that it was anything which contained silver. The necklace Terris had given him, lying on the dresser. The frame of a picture. A mirror on the wall and a small one inside a compact inside of a drawer. He could see through to it, because the drawer wasn't real, but the silver was. The keyboard of the computer glowed, and when Miles touched it, the keys melted away, revealing tiny silver circuits.

The great silver phallus glowed too, hidden deep within the nest of his clean underwear.

"Silver," Miles whispered. "Everything silver, I can see. But why? What am I to do with it?"

As if they had been waiting for this question, the pieces of silver lifted up from their places and began to drift toward the center of the room. The picture frame shattered, forming a silver needle and a long line of silver string; it threaded itself and began to sew Miles's torn clothing back together. The circuits of the keyboard hovered like glinting fireflies in the air. The mirrors glided beneath them like plates. The necklace wound itself around Miles's neck.

The phallus drifted eerily toward him, then without pausing made a turn at Miles's hip, heading for the not-yet sewn gap in his silver trousers.

Miles backed away from it, waving his hands. "No." He bumped into the mirror, then tangled some of the circuits in his hair; when he stopped to bat them away, he felt the cold tip of the phallus nudge him, and he yelped and jumped back, covering himself.

"No!" he shouted. "No, I don't want—"

Harry.

Miles stopped but kept his hands over his backside.

The beast. Your Harry. You must go back to him. You must wear it for your own protection, and for his.

The voice was musical and soft. Miles glanced around the room. "Are you Terris?"

The musical sound flared briefly dissonant. *No.*

Miles frowned. "Then who are you?"

There was a shimmer before him, and he watched the flute appear. Then, to his astonishment, he saw it transform: it shimmered and grew as Miles watched, becoming a tall, thin, very beautiful man.

The ghost-man. Except this time he was not ghostly at all, but very real. He was here, actually here in this dream place with Miles.

Miles caught the exquisite, perfect beauty of him and backed away. *Faerie.* This man was a faerie.

"Only half," the man said. "My mother is fey; my

father is human. I have the appearance and the abilities of the faerie, but my soul is human. My name is Murali."

His voice was very like a flute, lilting and quiet. Every phrase seemed to contain a song. Miles realized that he could very easily be hypnotized by it and very likely already was.

"Why are you a flute? Harry said you are the enemy of the Lord of Dreams. Are you in hiding?"

Murali laughed, the sound like an arpeggio. "No, I am not the enemy of the Lord of Dreams. I am his lover."

"Lover?"

Murali nodded. "I suppose I should say that I *was* his lover. We quarreled a long time ago, and I left him, though I had intended initially to come back. I went to Terris, asking him to help me hide. I meant him to transform me into something Almos could not find, and since my name means 'flute', a silver flute seemed appropriate. But Terris was just learning magic, and he made an unfortunate mistake. There is a condition to my release, one which, I am afraid, Almos cannot meet. Until someone does, enchanted I remain."

Miles frowned. This wasn't the story Terris had shown him at all. He had lied, even in that vision.

Murali laughed. "But how could you expect differently? He is fey. He does not think of you, only of himself. He cannot. None of them can."

"Then how could you love the Lord of Dreams?"

Murali shrugged. "My half-human heart is as much a mystery as yours. Why do you crave acceptance? Why do you long for power? Why are you so angry about the loss of a life which was so poisonous to you? Why can you not see that you are living in a paradise, that you have gifts whole worlds ache to know? Why not— because your heart has fixed itself on dreams, just as all human hearts do. I loved Almos because my heart chose him. Nothing the human heart does is rational. It is all a mad, mad dream. But the difference between the desires of you and I, Miles, and that of Almos or even Terris are that our dreams can become reality. At best a faerie heart can be a shade of love."

Murali stepped closer to Miles, and Miles realized he could see through him. He wasn't truly there, just a projection of him was. "You must take the silver from this room—your sacred space—inside of you. It will protect you from the beast that has claimed your Harry's mind."

"I have to take a phallus into my ass to protect myself?" Miles snapped.

Murali raised a ghostly silver eyebrow. "Would you rather take the beast?"

Miles flashed back to his near rape. Fear mingled with regret and frustration. "Is he truly lost?"

"Only you may decide that."

"How?"

"Ewart—Harry, as you say—has named you as his lover. We will find out now if he is right."

"What do you mean, he's named me as my lover?" *Ewart. That's his real name. I kind of like Harry better.* Miles shook himself back to attention. "Wait—are you telling me you think *I* can break this curse?"

Murali shrugged. "It's possible. Just because Ewart has been wrong so many times before doesn't mean that he is wrong this time too."

"Before?" Hot jealousy rushed through Miles. "You mean I'm not his first 'beloved'?"

Murali looked amused, but Miles noticed the softness that came over his face, as opposed to Terris's amusement. "The beast is born of Ewart's lonely heart. He loves everything living that crosses his path. All but poor Almos, which is why he won't release him. Almos is very vain."

So I'm not special. The thought was more disappointing than it should have been. "How does Terris fit into this?"

"I told you. Terris was imprisoned by Almos for transforming me."

Suddenly Miles understood. "That's why he keeps trying to seduce me. If Harry—Ewart—gets to me first, Terris loses his way out. Either Harry has a lover or Terris has his slingshot."

"Or Almos has another feast and watches both Ewart and Terris despair. In every instance to date, this is what has happened. I do what I can, but Terris's enchantment is quite good. Only one act may break it."

"And that act is?" Miles prompted.

Murali wagged his finger at him. "I'd like to break my enchantment, too, if you please. If I tell you, you will be unable to try and help me."

"Then how am I going to break it?"

"By being clever and by following your heart. You've done better than any other so far. Who knows? You might make it, this time."

"You sound rather blasé about the whole thing."

"Oh, I'm eager to have it over with, yes," Murali assured him. "But I have enough fey in me to keep from too much despair."

"And how do you explain Terris, then?"

"Almos can be very cruel, and he has been especially so to Terris for some time. But this is enough of your questions. You must go to Ewart, and you must take the beast from him."

"And how do you propose I do that? Or is this also part of my little quest?"

"You fill him with silver, of course." Murali gave him a curious look. "Didn't you see what happened to his hands when he tore at your silver clothing?"

"But he bled! And anyway, how am I supposed to get the silver in him?"

"He will bleed, yes. But he will transform, and that is what matters. As for how you get it into him—that's quite simple. You will take the silver into your body here, now. And then you will deposit it inside of him."

"But how—" Miles stopped. His jaw fell open.

"Into either his mouth or his anus, as you prefer."

"And how do you propose I get him to let me 'deposit' it? Promise to let him rape me after?"

"Oh, that would never work. You may need to let him put *his* seed in *you*, first. He'll be calmer after that."

Miles twitched. "But he's so huge!"

"Miles, there honestly isn't time for your foolishness. Will you do this, or shall I send you home?" When Miles sputtered in panic, Murali sighed and reached into his pocket. "Here. Will this ease your fears at all?"

Miles looked down at the small vial of what appeared to be oil in Murali's hand. "Is this some sort of super-faerie lube?"

This seemed to amuse him. "You might say that. Here." He made a circular motion with his finger. "Turn around, and I'll show you."

At this point there seemed no reason to object. Miles turned around, bent over, undid the ties to his trousers, and pulled them down.

Murali patted his naked rump. "There, you see? Everything is so much better when you're agreeable."

"Sure." Miles started when he heard the squirt of the oil into Murali's hand, then again when he felt the strange pressure of a fingertip against his hole. He pushed against it and gasped in pleasure as it slipped inside. It was warm and soft, and it made his insides burn in a very nice way.

"Oh," he gasped, and opened more for Murali.

"You're lovely," Murali pushed deeper. "So warm."

Miles groaned. Murali's finger felt barely there, but the oil was decidedly present. It gave him the strangest sensation of swelling, but it felt as if he were opening too. He felt more opened than he'd ever been before, in fact. When Murali added one finger, then another, and then another, Miles didn't even wince. He just moaned, pushed back against him, begging for more.

He felt a silky tongue slide up his naked cheek. "So *delightful*, Miles. Would you like me to show you how well you'll be able to accommodate Ewart? Shall I show you how pleasurable this oil will make it for you?"

All Miles could offer in answer was a grunt. Murali laughed, a wicked faerie laugh. Then he paused, withdrew, tucked his thumb inside his fist—and pushed inside.

Now it was Miles who sang. His face was red, and he was panting, and his head exploded as he felt Murali's slender arm sliding deep inside him, brushing his fist—*his whole fist*—against his prostate. He had never done this. Never. He had feared this above all kinky acts, and now here he was, with a half-faerie, half-human's enchanted fist buried deep within him, greased by magic lube. It aroused him like little else ever had, and soon his musical cries turned to grunts, and he huffed, waiting for Murali to take him all the way to the edge and over into ultimate pleasure.

But just when he was getting close, Murali withdrew. Miles cried out, then groaned again as the silver phallus was slipped snugly inside him. It seemed bigger than it had been before.

Murali kissed Miles's lower back as he cinched the strap in place. "You should know that even with this you will have some pain. Ewart is a beast all the way, and he will not be easy inside you. You may tear, despite all we have done."

The thought made Miles nauseous. "I don't want to *tear*."

"It won't be like you're thinking. No worse than some of your drunken bouts. Certainly no worse than a woman in childbirth." When Miles made a strangled sound, Murali patted his rump.

"I'm going to send you to him as soon as I put the silver inside you."

"How—?" Miles asked, voice still passion-rough, and then the silver shimmered in the air before him, he gasped, and in a puff, it rushed into his mouth.

"Silver vapor," Murali said, tugging his pants back into place.

Miles gagged and coughed, but the vapor was already seeping into his bloodstream. "Poisonous," he rasped.

"Yes, unfortunately, quite so to you. But I think I managed to give you just enough to only make you slightly bumbling. When you come inside him, try not to spill, please."

Miles tried to stand, but with the huge phallus, he could only make it halfway up. He grunted against the sensual pressure of the dildo. "But how—"

"You can get a little of it inside him with your saliva," Murali advised, "but you'll need to keep your cock deep inside his throat or anus when you make the true deposit. But I'd give the saliva a try; it might calm him so that he won't be so vicious when he takes you. The semen will do most of the work. It needs to get deep within his system, and an orgasm will help, too—the energy. He needs a great deal of silver, so don't waste it. I shudder to think what he'd be like if you went halfway."

"It has to be my semen?" Miles repeated, incredulous.

Murali shrugged. "Or your blood."

Miles whimpered.

Murali stroked his backside in a conciliatory gesture. "Would you like to call it off?"

It felt like a challenge. Miles was sure it was. Could he actually go home, he wondered? Would he be able to leave this that easily? And the answer came quickly: no. He shook his head.

Murali gave him one last caress. "Ready?"

Miles nodded again, then exhaled. His head spun from the silver. He thought of all the health risks inherent with silver vapor, and he wondered if it was going to be a race to see what killed him, Harry's lovemaking or Murali's cure.

"Good luck." Murali kissed him, and then he was gone.

The room rippled and changed, and the next thing

Miles knew, he was in the dungeon room, which stank more than ever of dead animal. He could see nothing, but he could hear the beast in the darkness. He gasped in fear and in pain from the hard object pushing into his ass as he tried to stand, and then great hands took him and crushed him with a roar against a hairy breast.

CHAPTER TEN

HARRY MADE NO attempt at conversation. Murmuring something that might have been Old English, he pressed Miles onto the floor and humped him.

Miles grabbed his face, then with a gag at the smell of him, fumbled for his mouth. Harry lived like a beast, and the evidence was in the blood matted in his beard and in his teeth; it was the most disgusting kiss Miles had ever had, and given some of his late-night encounters in Atlanta, that was a statement. But he shut down his revulsion and focused on thrusting as much of his tongue inside of Harry's mouth as he could, as deep as he could, as long as he could.

The gesture seemed to please Harry, and it did calm him somewhat, though it also made him grip Miles's arms harder. When Harry began to cry out from the pain of touching the silver cloth, Miles pulled back long enough to tug it over his head, then resumed the kiss again.

It was sweeter this time, or his mind had worked it out that he could believe it was so. However it happened, this time he was not feigning his enthusiasm as he laced his tongue around Harry's. It helped that Harry's thumbs were rubbing roughly against Miles's nipples and that his great cock was pushing against Miles's belly, but when his balls pressed too hard against Miles's trousers, Harry withdrew in pain again.

"It's okay," Miles said, breathless. With only a little hesitation, he tossed off his pants. "They're gone." He opened his arms nervously. "Come back, Harry."

"*Gástlufu.*" Harry crawled hesitantly forward. *Beloved.*

"Yes, *gástlufu.*" Miles took Harry's mouth once more.

He groaned as he felt Harry's great cock against his own, and he arched and moaned as Harry's fur-covered chest rubbed against his hairless, slender one. He'd never been with a hairy man before, ever. He always had gone for slight men, like himself. Slight, caustic men. He wouldn't have had two seconds for a brutish bear. Now he was panting beneath the bear of bears, unbuckling a monster of a dildo hurriedly as he willingly drew back his legs, pulled the phallus out, and made himself ready for Harry to enter him.

Even with the oil and Murali's preparation, as the faerie had warned, it still hurt when Harry thrust inside, and Miles cried out in pain, tears running out of his eyes as the beast began to rut inside him. But the fey oil quickly did its work, and soon he was purring and pushing back against Harry's cock, not to expel it but to take it deeper.

"Harry," Miles rasped, clutching at his shoulders. "Oh Harry!"

Harry fucked Miles like he had never been fucked before, pushing Miles's legs back so far they burned from the stretch, and Harry rutted like—well, like a beast inside of Miles. Harry grunted, he roared, and he pushed that monstrous organ deeper inside Miles than anything had ever been, deeper and harder than Murali's fist had gone, deeper than the phallus, deeper than even Miles's most wicked imagination. He felt so full, so stretched, and when Harry rubbed his pelvis in a circle and stimulated his prostate, he felt so horny he thought he would blow up if he didn't come. But he couldn't, not without wasting the silver. Gritting his teeth, Miles forced himself to hold back and simply lay there as the beast slaked his long-pent lust inside of him.

At last, with a cry that shook the dungeon, Harry came. Great warmth flooded Miles, moving deep into his bowels, oozing out of him onto the floor. They both gasped and clutched at one another, and then, too spent to do anything else, they collapsed into each other, Harry's great horned head resting on Miles's shoulder.

Miles turned his face and kissed one of Harry's horns. "It's all right. It's going to be all right. I promise."

Harry clutched convulsively at Miles's shoulders, making no move to rise. The beast, for the moment, had been slaked. Miles could even believe, as he lay there breathless beneath the beast, that some of the man had returned. He clutched at Harry's horns. He hoped so. He didn't think he could hold off from coming much longer.

Miles took no chances, though. Gently nudging Harry aside, he started to slide from beneath him.

Harry grunted and reached for him, keeping himself buried inside.

"Please," Miles murmured. He thrust his pelvis at Harry, trying to indicate he wanted to move away. But Harry only growled and held him fast. Miles hissed at the friction against his erection and tried again.

Then he gasped and held very still. Harry huffed against his neck, wriggling his hips until he was buried deep again. Miles shuddered, then fell back against the floor.

"Oh God! What *is* that?" he gasped, voice still shaking. "Fuck—Harry, what did you do to me?"

Harry huffed against his neck, no longer moving. Miles tried a few more times to free himself, but he couldn't. Then comprehension dawned.

A knot. Harry was a beast in every way. Harry's penis had a knot.

Miles cried out. "Oh my God, Harry!"

Harry nuzzled Miles's neck and gripped his shoulders. "Miles."

Miles panicked. "Harry, you have to let me go because I—" Then he got a good look at Harry's mouth, and eyes, and nose, and ears. Blood was pouring from them in increasingly thick streams.

Oh shit, Miles thought, just before Harry began to convulse.

Everything was such a mess. Harry was moving again, his cock buried deep, and even though Miles wanted to focus on helping Harry, the friction pushed him over the edge. With no warning, he came all over his own stomach and into the thick tufts of Harry's chest.

"No!" Miles cried, once he was spent. He reached between them, gathered what semen he could find, and smeared it as best he could past Harry's lips. "Harry— swallow it, Harry!"

But mostly Harry was drooling it back out. Miles tried kissing it back in, but it was no use. He scooped up more, but at this point it could be hardly worth anything.

I shudder to think of what he'd be like if you went halfway. That's what Murali had said. Miles was fairly sure that's what he was witnessing now.

Or you could use your blood.

Miles drew his hand up to his mouth and bit hard into his thumb. He yelped in pain, but when he drew back, the skin wasn't broken. He started to try again, then looked into Harry's mouth, at his jagged teeth, then reached up and slashed hard.

He cried out, then stuck his thumb deep into Harry's throat and squeezed the rent flesh against Harry's tongue.

He wasn't sure how much thumbs could bleed, or how equivalent blood was to semen, so he kept it there, dripping, all the time whispering, pleading, begging Harry to suckle it, to take enough to heal. But Harry only rasped, bleeding still, and it wasn't long before Miles's pleas became sobs.

"Please work," he whispered, squeezing his thumb harder. "Please, please work!"

But Harry bled, and bled, and so did Miles, and all the while the silver hung inside him like lead. He began to grow dizzy, and then so sleepy.

He blinked, long and languid.

When he opened his eyes, he was in the castle again, lying on Terris's silver-sheeted bed. Terris lay naked beside him and looking down curiously at Miles.

Miles blinked, remembered, then cried out in despair. "No—*no!*"

Terris pouted. "That's not usually how you greet me, Miles."

Miles sat up, shoving the silken sheets away. "Harry—where is Harry?"

"Rotting in his dungeon, I assume." Terris lay back on the bed and threaded his hands behind his head. "Don't worry. The old goat can't die. The Lord won't allow it. Whatever happened to him, he'll recover."

"But I wanted him to *heal.*" Miles stumbled out of the bed and headed for the door. He fell twice along the way. "I have to find him. I have to finish." He fell a third time, and this time he couldn't get up until Terris came and helped him. "Why am I so dizzy?"

"You lost a great deal of blood. I've only just staunched the bleeding now. And you have enough silver in you to kill most mortals. Honestly, darling, suicide was not necessary. You could have just gone home. You'd have forgotten me eventually. All humans do."

"I wasn't trying to kill myself. I was trying—" He broke away from Terris and fell immediately, then cried out in frustration. "Damn it!"

Terris laughed. "Miles, you silly creature. What is this about, honestly? Don't tell me all this is some half-baked plan to save that beast!"

"It's not half-baked!" Miles whirled on Terris, then had to brace himself against the bed to stop the room from spinning. "I met Murali, Terris! I know all about it! I know that I can save Harry, and I'm going to!"

"Harry?" Terris frowned, then choked on more laughter. "*Ewart?* Oh, *Miles!*" He held his sides as he guffawed. "Miles—oh, darling, Murali is a hopeless prankster! He's one of the Lord's agents! Darling—oh,

no, don't pout at me! It's not my fault you're so gullible!"

"I'm not gullible!" Miles shot back. "You lie! You
lie all the time! You only care about yourself! You'd
leave me like you did him if it came to that—and I'm
not going to let it go on!"

"How do you know it's me lying," Terris asked silk-
ily, "and not Murali?"

And as Miles looked into Terris's eyes, his beautiful
silver eyes, he realized that he didn't know. That there
was no way to verify what was truth and what was lie.
He might not be able to save Harry. He might not be
able to save anyone, not even himself. This could all be
one big faerie game, and he was the loser no matter
what he did.

But most important of all, he discovered he didn't
care.

Terris realized it, too, and he drew back in shock.
Then he made his face carefully blank. But it was too
late; Miles had seen his reaction.

"I don't care," Miles said aloud, just to drive the
point home, both to Terris and to himself. "If this is all
a joke, if you're all mocking me? *Fine.* I don't care. I'm
going after him anyway."

Terris arched an elegant eyebrow. "Someone's full
of silver, I see."

"Yeah." Miles stumbled sideways as he gestured at
Terris. "Full of silver. Delusional, confused. Stumbling.
Half-poisoned, all to save some guy I barely know,

whom I've had one conversation with, and who I've just let fuck me with a cock with a fucking hook on the end. And apparently I'm bleeding to death."

"I stopped that part." Terris spoke idly, but there was a strange focus in his voice. Miles had his attention.

He wished he knew what the hell to do with it.

"I'm going to find Harry." He headed to the door again.

"You won't find him that way, Miles."

"I'm not listening to you, liar."

Miles fell down again. Terris caught him. "Miles." There was a weariness to his voice, and a resignation. "Miles—you have to stop. You'll find nothing out this door. You won't even find a door if you look more carefully."

Miles frowned over his shoulder, and his eyes widened as he saw that Terris was right. "What the hell? Where did it go?"

"It didn't go anywhere," Terris said. He was strangely patient. "It was never there."

"I walked through it." Miles frowned. "Didn't I?"

"No." Terris sighed and gestured to the room. "None of this is here, Miles. It never was."

"I don't understand," Miles said.

"I told you that I was a prisoner of the Lord of Dreams. I *showed* you. You felt the cold. You felt my prison. Didn't you wonder how I could be in prison and yet follow you around through your life, how I could take you through the Lord's castle?"

"But—" Miles said, then cut himself off in confusion.

Terris looked sad. "I said, several times, that it was all a dream."

He waved his hand, and the dream faded.

It was the dungeon again, but a different part. This was not Harry's great cavern but a small anteroom, almost like a tomb. In the center of the room was a long marble box, strapped tight with iron bars.

It was the coldest room Miles had ever been in that wasn't encased in ice.

"What is this place?" Miles asked. "Why are we here?"

"We have always been here." Terris looked down at the marble box, his expression full of pain. "I have, anyway."

Miles looked at the box again, noting the man-sized shape of it. He also noted the iron. That had been in Julie's notes: faeries hated iron.

A strange sorrow welled inside of Miles. "No," he said, but he wasn't even sure yet what he was denying.

"I'm afraid the answer is yes. That's me, inside there. I have iron spikes digging into my heart, my mouth, and my brain, and of course, my genitals. I worked the one out of my stomach a few centuries in, but that was the only one I could manage. After that, I focused on sending my mind outside. It seemed a better use of my talents."

Miles shook his head in sick bewilderment. "But—

how?"

"How what? How did my Lord do this to me? He snapped his fingers and ordered his soldiers to bind me, Miles, that's how. They drove in the spikes, and they laughed while they did it, too, especially when I pleaded for mercy. That's how it's done."

Miles could envision it, and it was awful. "How—how did you send your mind out?"

"With practice. I was only an amateur magician, but I had a strong base from which to build. I practiced inside my prison, and then I gathered bits of silver to help make my projection solid outside of this room. It repels the Lord of Dreams, you see, because dreams are like parasites, living off souls, and silver kills parasites. But with the Lord of Dreams, it's more that he can't see anyone cased in silver. It helps, too, that silver has so many other uses." He glanced sideways at Miles. "But you truly have had too much. Don't take in anymore, or even I won't be able to save you."

Miles didn't care about that. "But where is Harry? He's not a dream. I know he isn't."

"He's here too. Just around the corner."

Miles started to leave, but Terris stopped him by grabbing his arm.

"I want to go to him," Miles said, trying to tug him away.

Terris held him fast. "You're already there, Miles. Think about it," he said when Miles frowned. "If I'm actually in the box, but I'm standing here talking to you, then I'm not real. And if I'm able to hold onto you, this isn't the real you, either."

Miles was lost. "Where am I, then?"

Terris looked hard into his eyes. "The Lord of Dreams won't let him go. You can still leave. He cannot."

"You're lying again," Miles shot back.

Terris shook his head. "The Lord will trick you, Miles. That's what faeries do. Trust nothing he says. Enjoy your moment with Ewart, but then it's over. Go home." He withdrew a silver pill from his pocket. "Squeeze this hard between your fingers. You'll fly straight home and forget all about us." He tucked the pill behind Miles's ear, but it wasn't there when he reached up to pull it away.

"Let me go to him," Miles demanded through clenched teeth.

"As I have said, you're already there."

The scene changed again. This time it was dark, and dank, and very cold. But Miles felt very warm, in part because his body was flushed with silver, and in part because he was in someone's arms.

"Miles—Miles—come back to me, Miles!"

Miles opened his eyes and looked up into a kind, handsome, bearded face. It was Harry. He was awake. He was alive.

He was a man.

"HARRY!" MILES REACHED up and touched his face tentatively, afraid he might not be real. He stroked his smooth, beautiful skin, and he laughed, his heart tight within his chest. "Harry—you're alive!"

"I could say the same for you," Harry replied gruffly. He stroked Miles's hair, looking worried. "You were so still and so pale. You still are. Your skin is gray, Miles."

"I took silver. I gave it to you because Murali said it would cure you, and he was right." He touched Harry's cheeks, his nose, his lips, still caught up in the wonder of his beauty. "Did you know your real name is Ewart? You're from England. Very, very old England."

"I don't remember any of it," Harry said, without concern. "I'm content to be your Harry." He cradled Miles's cheek in his hand and looked at him with a stunned expression. "Why did you do all this for me? I'm moved, but—Miles, why?"

Why did everyone keep asking him this? "Because it isn't right, what happened to you," Miles replied. "Because you deserve to be free."

"He's not going to let me go, Miles. You need to leave before he finds out you've restored me. I'm grateful for this moment, but it will be fleeting."

"I'm not leaving without you," Miles said.

Harry pressed a kiss against Miles's forehead. "I'm not going to argue with you, not now. Not when I'm finally holding you in my arms."

Miles shut his eyes against the tenderness of the

kiss and slid his hands down Harry's chest. Harry's naked chest, he amended, sliding his fingers through the soft down. He skimmed the slope of his shoulders, too, and the lines of muscle on his arms. He was so fit, which surprised him, but then he realized that would make sense, if he'd been spending all this time running and hunting in faerie land. He looked, in fact, much like he always had, except he didn't have horns, and he didn't have quite so much hair. He was still a hairy man, yes—he still had a beard, and it was longer than Miles would normally care for, but it suited him, as did the curly mess of brown hair that covered his head and curled around his ears. But he was a man now, with a man's body, and a man's mind. When Miles looked into his eyes, he didn't see a wild, mad beast in pain—he saw Harry.

"You're so beautiful," Miles whispered, still touching him.

Harry smiled, stroked Miles's chin, then leaned down and kissed him softly. Even the brief touch of those soft lips was enough to make Miles melt.

"You're the one who is beautiful, your soul as well as your body." His face shuttered. "Miles, I'm so sorry I hurt you."

"I don't care—it was worth it to help you." Miles skimmed his hands up Harry's body again, his thumbs pausing at Harry's nipples. "I don't hurt anymore, anywhere. I feel a little dizzy from the silver, but seeing you like this—Harry, I could fly." He hesitated, then added, his eyes still on Harry's chest, "I love you, Harry."

His heart was pounding nervously, and it fluttered when he felt Harry's tender kiss at his temple. He shut his eyes.

"Why?" Harry whispered, his voice soft, and gruff, sounding almost like the beast's again. "*How?* I was a monster—"

Miles pressed his fingers against Harry's mouth, quieting him. "I was too. I just didn't look like one on the outside." He traced the seam of Harry's lips. "I was so selfish, so self-centered."

"That isn't true," Harry said, defensive. "You were kind to me from the moment you saw me. You keep coming back here for me. You've *saved me*, Miles, in more ways than one."

Miles tipped his head back and looked him in the eye. "But it was you that taught me I could be that way. So we're even, because you saved me too."

Harry smiled, then briefly nipped at one of Miles's fingers. "We should find a way to thank each other."

Oh, Miles had some pretty specific ways in mind. But he glanced nervously around the room. "How often does the Lord of Dreams come to you?"

"A few times a century." Harry's hand drifted down Miles's naked back. "And I just saw him a few hours ago."

"But he knows I'm here, and he's looking for me," Miles pointed out. Harry's fingers drifted toward the cleft of his backside, and he gasped. "*Harry.*"

"He still has a hold on me. I'll know when he's close by." Harry's head dipped, and he placed a soft, open-mouthed kiss against Miles's neck. "Right now he's on the other side of the universe."

"I want to get you out of here," Miles whispered, but he tipped his head to the side to give Harry better access.

Harry nibbled his way down Miles's collarbone. "How are you planning to do that?"

"I don't know yet." Miles shuddered and let his head fall back as Harry's fingers found his nipple and pinched with a force that both surprised and aroused him. "*Oh.*"

"Mmm. If you don't mind, I'll just keep myself occupied here while you do your thinking."

His mouth closed over Miles's other nipple, suckling, then nipping at the peak as he tormented the other with his fingers. Miles gasped and clutched at his hair. "I can't think when you do that!"

"Then don't think. Miles, you've seen me shamed and you've seen me broken. You've known me as a man and as a beast. If you can free me from the Lord of Dreams, I will go anywhere with you. But what I want right now is to know you as the man I am, whole and sane and strong once more. I want to love you as that man, so that the Harry you say you love is not a figure of pity but of strength, and desire."

"I do love you."

"Then let me love you back." Harry lowered his mouth again.

Miles arched toward Harry.

In so many ways, this felt like the first time. Instead of seducing the beast-Harry into a kiss and trying to manipulate their coupling so that he didn't get hurt, Miles was now yielding, opening to the same man, who in many ways was just as forceful and strong as the beast. His hand skidded down and took Harry's cock into his hand. *Big* cock, still. But Harry's mind was here now, which had the odd effect of allowing Miles to let his go. He would call Murali and Terris and demand they tell him how to set Harry free, but for now he would give himself this release, this moment with his lover, in case he failed and it was the only one he had.

He ran his fingers through Harry's hair, over his ears, and down his back. When Harry slid his mouth down Miles's sternum, anchoring his palms against Miles's hips, Miles opened his legs and invited him in, thrusting toward Harry's mouth as his lips parted wide. But Harry only teased Miles's cock, trailing his tongue down the thick vein at its back. He suckled Miles's balls, then pushed Miles's legs, bending them at his knees, pressing his heels against the backs of his thighs as he opened Miles to his gaze.

For a long time, he simply stared down at Miles, and Miles held still, letting him.

"I remembered this," he said gruffly, still staring at the puckered opening. "Even when the madness returned, I remembered you, standing inside your circle, displaying yourself for me. It filled me with such lust, but with such tenderness, too, that you would do this for the beast that I was. Even that act alone would have been enough to lift my spirit for seven centuries, Miles. But now—"

He let go of one of Miles's legs, reaching down to touch Miles's anus, which was already gaping eagerly, waiting to take him in. He pressed his thumb against it, and they both shuddered.

"Oh, Miles, I cannot tell you what a joy it is to simply look at you. To touch you." His thumb pressed carefully inside, and his eyes darkened. "So hot inside. Sweet heaven, Miles, but I want to bury myself in you. I want to taste you, touch you. I want to hear you cry out as I claim you. I want to feel you convulse around me as I drive you to your pleasure."

Miles was very dizzy now, but it had little to do with the silver. "That," he whispered, grabbing his thighs and spreading himself farther open. "Do all that to me, Harry—please!"

Harry gave him a wicked, beast-like grin. Then he bent his head, pulled his thumb down hard, and thrust his tongue in beside it.

Harry made love to Miles like a man who had taken several thousand years to anticipate the pleasure. He took his time with every aspect of his attentions, and he was achingly thorough. He spent what felt like years at Miles's ass, fingering him deep, stretching him with several fingers, pausing occasionally to insert one from each hand, opening him wide, and fucking him roughly with his tongue. He returned to this often, sometimes switching from tender, exploring caresses to an almost brutal claiming with so little warning that Miles cried out in ecstatic surprise every time. But he liked, too, when Harry would suckle his cock, one hand toying with Miles's balls while the other pushed as many fingers deep within him as Miles's increasingly elastic ass would handle. When Miles couldn't stand it any longer, he tugged Harry sideways to lie beside him, and as Harry continued his erotic exploration of the land below Miles's waist, Miles stroked Harry's cock and balls, then took his beautiful shaft deep into his mouth. It was so big, so wide; he moaned when the thickness slipped into his throat, and he suckled hard, clutching at Harry's muscled cheeks as he tried to take more and more of his lover.

He soon had himself worked into a frenzy, and when he felt Murali's faerie lotion on the ground beside him—apparently Murali was still nudging things along, because Miles hadn't brought it—he didn't pause, just squeezed some into his hand and used it to work his own fingers inside Harry.

Harry groaned appreciatively, but didn't let Miles linger there long. Withdrawing from Miles's mouth, Harry sat up, taking the oil from him. "I'm going to use this on you. I want you to know nothing but pleasure this time."

Miles held himself open, his arousal thickening as he watched Harry grease his fingers, then push two of them inside. Miles gasped in pleasure, pushed against them to draw them deeper, and pulled his legs open wider.

"More," he whispered.

Harry gave him a third and pushed deeper, twisting his fingers, making Miles groan.

"More," Miles pleaded again.

Harry added some grease, then gave Miles what he wanted. Miles shut his eyes and tipped his head back, reveling at the fullness inside his body. He heard Harry's short, arousal-roughened breaths, and they drove him higher and higher inside his own need. He could feel the anchor of Harry's thumb between his cheeks, but the oil was heating him, driving him higher. It wasn't enough.

"More," he demanded. Harry hesitated. He pushed a little deeper, moved a little faster, but it wasn't enough. Miles shook his head and pushed up toward him, desperate. "Harry—Harry, *please!*"

Harry tucked in his thumb and pushed deep, deep inside.

Miles cried out, gasping, keening in exquisite pleasure as Harry thrust as Murali had, but it was different with Harry. Murali had been preparing him. Harry was loving him.

I love you, Miles wanted to cry out, but he could only grunt.

"I want to put my cock inside you, Miles," Harry growled, pushing his fist in deep. "I want to spend myself inside you."

Still unable to speak, Miles nodded.

There was a brief, agonizing moment when Harry withdrew—and then he was pushing inside Miles again, pressing in and down, stretching Miles again, burying himself until their chests were pressed together, flesh to flesh. For a moment they held like that, fully joined, straining, gasping. Then Harry reached between them, took Miles's cock inside his fist, and began to move.

Miles shut his eyes and gave himself to his lover. But where the other time had been a fucking, a slaking, this time it was a union and a claiming. It was beautiful, a total surrender, Miles yielding, Harry thrusting, both of them giving to one another until there was no beginning and no end. And it was too much, too intense; despite the lingering before, neither of them could last now, and Miles bucked and spurted between their bodies just before Harry groaned and buried deep, filling Miles with his warm, thick seed.

Harry gasped, bucked once more, and collapsed into Miles's willing arms.

"That was incredible." Harry dragged a weary kiss against Miles's throat. "*You* are incredible."

Miles smiled and kissed him back. "Let's rest a bit, and we'll do it again."

Harry laughed wickedly, drawing his hand down Miles's side. Then, abruptly, he tensed. He withdrew and rose to his knees, his face white with fear.

"He's here—no warning at all! I didn't even feel him drawing close!" He gripped Miles's arm. "You must go! Hide! Don't let him find you!"

"I won't leave you," Miles said, as they scrambled to their feet. He looked around the room. "Murali—Terris! Help me!"

"You must go!" Harry cried again. "You must escape!"

There is no escape for either of you, a great voice boomed inside their heads. *And there never will be.*

The dungeon rushed with wind, then filled with bright, bright light and the sharp scent of summer night, and when the light faded, the Lord of Dreams stood in the center of the room, bearing down upon them.

CHAPTER ELEVEN

For if you leave me, lover, the truth I must face:
my life is just misery, just loss, just disgrace.
Please, lover! Please take me on wing or on sigh!
For if you do not claim me, then I will not die.

T HE LORD OF Dreams filled the dungeon. He
stood no taller than either Harry or Miles, but his
glamour pressed against the room, dominating both the
space and the minds within. *I am the whole world*, his
mere presence declared, and it wasn't a statement or a
challenge: it was a truth. There was nothing outside the
Lord of Dreams when you were within his sphere, and
when he noticed you, you were helpless.

Right now he noticed Miles.

Miles had been able to cast his eyes down, but it
was like averting his eyes from a furnace: the heat still
burned him. He could feel the Lord of Dreams moving
his gaze across him, sensing his existence but not able
to see him properly because of the silver. If the Lord
hadn't been seeking him, Miles thought he might have

escaped. But without Murali, without Terris, now that the Lord bore down on him, there was no way out, even with the silver.

"Who is this creature?" the Lord of Dreams demanded. "Who is this who is here but is not?" The intensity of his gaze shifted to Harry. "What magician have you brought into your lair, and from where did you get the arrogance to think you could so defy me?"

It took every ounce of Miles's will to keep from calling out, from throwing himself at the Lord's feet and confessing, not from fear, but by sheer compulsion. Which was why he was all the more impressed when Harry tipped his head back, looked the faerie straight in the face, and lied.

"There is no one here, My Lord. Someone came and cast a spell on me, but I did not see who they were, and they have already gone."

"*Liar!*" the Lord of Dreams roared, making the dungeon shake.

Miles swayed on his feet and staggered to keep from falling over.

Harry swayed, too, but he moved with the faerie's rhythm, and he stood fast. He said nothing.

"He's filled you with silver, whoever he is," the Lord snarled. "Not enough to hide you, but enough to make you belligerent. Well, human, you'll sweat that out soon enough. Don't get too smug in your sanity. You know it's only harder on you when you have this far to fall." His tone lightened a little, and he sounded almost pleased. "You haven't been this whole, in fact, in a long, long time. I might start paying more attention to you again. You're such an interesting diversion as you lose your mind."

"As it pleases you, of course, My Lord." Harry bowed.

Miles gritted his teeth and clenched his hands at his sides, but he kept his head down.

Even that, though, had been a mistake, he soon realized—the Lord of Dreams jerked to attention, a gesture Miles could not see but still felt. The awareness came upon him again.

"By the light—he's still *here*! Entirely invisible, and he's *angry* with me!" The Lord laughed. "Ooh, he's *furious* with me—and terrified, all at the same time. How *delicious*. Ewart, you scamp! Are you harboring a *human*?"

"I harbor no one, My Lord," Harry said, still preternaturally calm.

The Lord of Dreams snorted. "You always did enjoy a loophole. Well, you're already becoming boring again, I'm sorry to say. I think it's time to pull Terris out of his stuffing, don't you? It might be amusing to see what my fair faerie has to say about all this."

Terris? Miles looked up as much as he dared, and saw the Lord of Dreams crossing the room toward a far wall, where Miles realized for the first time there was a door. Hardly realizing he was doing so, he drifted across the room after the faerie, slipping behind the door just in time before it closed. He stood motionless in the shadows, watching as the Lord of Dreams waved a hand and made gray, shadowy servants appear from thin air. They shuffled forward like wraiths, and with skeletal hands undid the iron bands that held the box together before they slid the heavy stone top aside.

"Don't look," said a mild, quiet voice beside his ear.

Miles turned and saw Terris there, but it was a faint, transparent Terris. He watched the box open with a closed, granite-like expression.

"I can't take much of a form with him in the room," Terris went on in the same tone, "but after hearing my tale, you should have already guessed that you won't like what you see of my body in its prison. It will upset you, which will only give him more power over you. It's bad enough that he was able to draw you into my room. Things will get black if you let him take this much further."

Miles wondered if he could whisper without being heard.

Terris shrugged. "Hardly necessary, since I can hear everything you're thinking. But yes, I think he'd hear you. You aren't very guarded under normal circumstances. Silver can only do so much."

I need more, Miles thought. *So I can resist him.*

"If I give you any more, you'll resist breathing. I'm already using considerable force to prop you up as it is. You're sweating silver, darling, you have so much inside you. It's a shame we're not near a mirror. You're going to make a very handsome older man."

Miles reached up and touched his hair self-consciously. Then, without meaning to, he turned back toward the center of the room just as the lid was lifted away. He thought he saw a pale gray foot, twitching.

Terris grabbed his face and wrenched it back. "You are so *weak*," he snapped. "You let anyone into your mind just for tapping on your skull, don't you?"

Did he? Miles tried to disprove this, to push everyone out in defiance, and the next thing he knew he was drifting, like a silver feather, to the ground.

"Idiot," Terris hissed as he propped him back up again. "Don't resist *me*. Resist *him*."

"I'm trying," Miles whispered, then realized he'd said it out loud and glanced at the Lord of Dreams in alarm. And saw his face.

It was over. Completely, totally, forever—over.

There was a moment that he wasn't enslaved, a little sliver of time where he saw it all and understood, in an academic way, that Terris had mimicked the Lord of Dreams all along, both in habit and in appearance, and that he had even been learning from his magical techniques. He understood the way and shape of all the illusions: Terris had never left his prison, but he had created a glamour of the mind in the same way that the Lord of Dreams created his glamour of a forest world. Miles suspected that above him he would find the same glittering castle through which Terris had led him, only the true palace would be bigger and grander and even more perfect. Terris had punctured that glamour, too, using silver he gathered sometimes from the very air around him to make a mirror, and he had used Harry as his bait, letting him out into leaky places in the world, to people who yearned for the sort of perfection faeries can provide. But this dungeon was real, not glamoured at all.

And neither was the Lord of Dreams.

That was his magic. Most faeries, including Terris, wore illusions, but the Lord of Dreams truly was this beautiful, this perfect. He was made, after all, out of the fantasies of mortals, of their wishes and yearnings, and he ruled them all, luring them into his land both in sleep and in their waking lives. To look him in the face was to see everything your heart hoped for, every secret longing fulfilled and reflected back to you. No human, no matter how much silver he carried, could turn away.

"Yes," the Lord of Dreams said, his voice so beautiful, so perfect, spilling from those lips that Miles longed to kiss, to touch, to simply stare at for the rest of his life, because nothing else would ever be as good or wonderful as this. He sighed and reached for him, and the Lord of Dreams reached back. "Yes, my child. I cannot see you, but I can feel you. Human. Sweet human, full of dreams. Give them to me, all of them, and I will show you your pleasure. I will give you what you have longed for."

Miles could see it. He could see all of it, and he

smiled as he reached out to take the faerie's hand, knowing that when he touched it he would feel the fire, and it would burn him so beautifully. He felt the silver melting away, out of his body, and he let it go, because he didn't need it, not with Him. He didn't need anything, and he never would, not ever again, if he could only touch that hand—

There was a flash before him, a silver light. For one second he saw Murali, smiling kindly at him. Then he saw nothing at all—nothing but himself. He drew back, and so did he, the image before him.

A mirror. He was looking into a mirror.

Terris was right—he was gray from head to toe. His hair glistened silver-white, and his skin had a metallic pallor, as did his lips, his nose, his teeth. He looked down at his hands and saw that his fingernails were silver, too, as if they had been painted.

There was a roar and a crash, and the mirror cracked.

It flew straight into Miles's eyes.

It hurt. It hurt *a lot*, and Miles shrieked in pain, clawing at his eyes to get it out, but it buried itself deep, and after a few seconds, it barely hurt at all. He lifted his head, wiping the blood away from his face—silver blood, he saw, glancing at his wet hands—and he looked up again at the faerie.

This time he screamed and backed away.

Through the shards of mirror, the Lord of Dreams was not a vision, but a nightmare. He was not tall and handsome and perfect. He was slight and stooped and thin, gaunt, distended—terrible. He was cold, and he was helpless, uglier than anything Miles had ever dreamed could be. He was waste. He was absence living, a yawning horror of a creature. He was made of dreams, yes: empty, impossible dreams, the echoes that hearts knew they needed to discard but could not bring themselves to toss away. He ate those dregs up and spun them back into beauty, but he himself was empty. Now that Miles saw, he was horrified. The Lord of Dreams was a living terror, containing nothing, existing of nothing, able only to suck out souls.

Miles turned away.

Harry was here, too, looking not at the Lord, but at Miles, heartsick until he saw Miles's face, and then he looked relieved. "Miles," he whispered, then fell silent as the Lord of Dreams raised a hand and Harry fell into silence.

"There is someone here," the faerie hissed. "Not Terris, and not my slave. Not the human. *Someone is helping it.* And when I find out who it is, I will show no mercy."

Terris drifted up beside Miles, looking alarmed. "Mirrors in your eyes. You'll never survive this." He touched Miles's silver skin and shook his head. "He's poured it into you. Half the flute, at least. No—by the stars, he's put it *all* in you! Murali's run mad. What good is this going to do?"

Miles didn't know, but he knew he was very, very

dizzy. He staggered backward, shaking his head. "I feel funny," he said. He sounded funny too. He sounded musical, like Murali. He looked across the room at Harry, who had gone still and quiet.

"The Lord of Dreams still has Ewart under his spell," Terris said gently. "He has never been able to be what Ewart desires, but he can still control him, as he's human."

"Why?" Miles said. He braced against the stone box for support. He glanced around absently, wondering where the gray servants had gone. "Why can't he be what Harry desires?"

"Because I put a spell on Ewart," Terris said, a little tersely. "I gave him a mirror and showed him his beloved, his true heart. That's all he's ever wanted, ever since."

Miles looked across the room at Harry, cowering calmly as the Lord of Dreams raged over him. "Is that me?" he asked quietly. "Am I his beloved?"

Terris snorted. "*Everyone* is his beloved. That's the trick, you see? Ewart loves whoever he sees. It was supposed to be me. I wasn't smart enough yet to realize it wouldn't work on a faerie."

"Oh." Miles felt suddenly hollow. "So—so no one can save Harry?"

"No," Terris said, distracted. "But he doesn't matter. He's no use to me."

"He is to me," Miles snapped. Then swayed.

"You're getting sicker." Terris flattened his lips and

shook his head. "Damn you, Murali, this is a *waste*."

"People are more than just useful." Miles's voice was growing faint. "We aren't entertainment, and we aren't vehicles of escape."

"Says the man who spent a decade angry with the world for not behaving as he wanted it to. 'I'm so much better than this.' You looked at the world and all you saw was what it could give you, what it could do for you, and most of all, what it *wasn't* giving you. It never occurred to you that you might be without because someone else needed something, or because you had something else instead. No, you were just like a fey, Miles. You looked at the world and knew it owed you, because you didn't see anything but what it could do for you."

"That's not true," Miles whispered, sick at heart because he knew that it was.

The Lord had stopped shouting at Harry and had come back over to the crypt. Miles gagged at the sight of the faerie lord, but the Lord of Dreams could not hear him now.

"I feel it," the faerie said, reaching out for Miles with a gaunt hand. "I don't know how it's resisting me, but I'll find it, and I'll turn it into another beast. I'll watch the pair of you rut together, then torture you to watch you howl. Just as soon as I *find* him—"

Miles staggered farther away, sliding farther down the box. Something brushed his hand, and he looked down.

"No!" Terris shouted, but it was too late. Miles had already seen.

There was a body in the stone box, but it could not be identified as a man. It was tortured and rotted, its flesh eaten away as if by acid, and where the iron stakes had been driven—which was pretty evenly every two to three inches—open wounds gushed black, sickly blood. It was a scene so gruesome it wouldn't have been allowed in a horror film. The gore wasn't the problem. It wasn't even that the body was twitching in a constant, helpless spasm.

The mirrors in Miles's eyes only further illuminated the despair, the pain, the stark suffering that the creature within experienced, would continue to know until the Lord of Dreams decided he'd had enough. Other faeries might have stopped it, but no one had come, and so it had not stopped. It had just gone on, and on, and on, a torture only a faerie could devise, and only a faerie could bear. But even on this creature for whom feelings were but dust on his clothing, the torture had begun to take its toll. The wraith standing beside Miles, the shard of Terris which had lured him here, which had flattered him and made love to him, which had seen so deeply into the heart of him—that part knew no pain.

The creature inside this box was now nothing but pain. And this creature was Terris too. The true Terris.

Something shifted inside Miles, a key turning in a lock. He felt Murali's cool hands on his shoulders, then heard a faint, soft tune as Murali's spell broke, un-locked by the gift of Miles's soul.

Like a key borrowed and no longer needed, Murali gave it right back, and with it came all the pain, all the sorrow, all the ache—his own and Murali's.

Miles was dimly aware that he sobbed, but mostly he knew he had to stop this, that what had been done to Terris was wrong beyond wrong. Reaching into the box, he dug his silver-coated fingers into the flesh and yanked out the iron stakes one by one. The gray serv-ants reappeared, hissing, but Miles only shouted at them and knocked them back and went on with his work.

Terris stood beside him, watching impassively.

"This isn't going to do any good," he said, curling his lip in disgust as a bloody iron spike flew past his platinum head. "It's not going to save your lover, and it doesn't matter much to me."

"It's your *body*." Miles pried out another stake.

The Lord of Dreams started and turned toward the box. Miles ignored him and continued to work.

"It's a mess. This body is no good to me now. Even when it's healed, it's going to remember that pain. I can't possibly live in it."

"You'll be a wraith forever, then?" Miles tossed out another spike.

"I'd *intended* to ride a human out of this universe," Terris said acidly, "but then someone had to go and swallow a lethal amount of silver."

"I'm not dead yet. Stop distracting me."

"What the devil is going on?" the Lord of Dreams demanded and stormed up beside Miles, walking right through Terris.

"And you—*shut up*," Miles snarled, then turned and drove an iron stake straight into the heart of the Lord of Dreams.

The Lord screamed and fell back, but Miles ignored him and went right back to working.

"Miles." This was Harry, approaching the box carefully, looking wary. "Miles—what are you doing?"

"Fixing things." Miles had everything out of the arms and the chest. He just had a few in the groin and two in the head that had squicked him out at first, but by this point, they didn't bother him at all. He had to do this. He had to finish this.

"I think he's gone insane." Terris turned to Harry with a sneer. "You'll have company."

Harry looked uneasy. "Miles, you've made the Lord of Dreams angry. You need to get out of here."

"Where am I going to go?" Miles dug his fingers into the flesh of Terris's groin. "Back to Summer Hill? Take Terris's silver pill and forget everything?" He yanked out the spike. "Go back to waiting for the world to fix itself for me? *Never.*" He aimed the spike at Terris's face. "I'm *not* like the fey. I don't expect the world to be there to serve me. I know it looks like that, but that isn't what I wanted. What I wanted was to not have to do the work. There's a big difference. I thought the world wasn't fair, and I was hurt because it wasn't fixing itself for me. Well, I'm done with that. I'm going to fix my own life. I'm going to fix what's wrong. Me. That's what I'm going to do. And I'm starting with this, because it's the most wrong thing I've ever seen."

"Miles," Harry said, even more desperate now. "Miles, he's getting up!"

Miles pulled the last stake out of Terris's head, then turned to face the Lord of Dreams, who he'd known was right behind him even without being told. He turned, full of rage, and raised the stake.

The Lord of Dreams hissed in fury, his horrible gaunt jaw gaping as he shouted at Miles.

"You stupid fool! You can't best me, no matter how much silver you take! I am the Lord of Dreams! I am invincible!"

"You're *nothing*!" Miles shouted, and he knew for the first time that it wasn't just him shouting. His voice was an angry flute now, and he knew that Murali was there, too. "You're nothing, and you've always been nothing. You're nothing more than the dreams you suck out of lives. I looked at you and saw a god, and then I saw you through the mirror of the silver, and I realized how stupid I'd been, how you'd hypnotized me just like everyone else, that I'd never loved you at all. I'd only been glamoured like the rest. You never loved me, not even in the horrible way any faerie loves another. So I ran, but you wouldn't let me go, not even then—not because you cared, but because you hated to be bested!"

Terris went still, and so did Harry. The Lord of Dreams blinked in surprise. "Murali?"

"You tortured Terris!" Miles cried, but he was just a vessel now, getting out of the way so Murali could have his moment at last. "He helped me, and you *tortured* him! He didn't have to do it, and it didn't give him anything at all—"

"—power," Terris said quietly.

Miles turned and looked at him. In the back of his head, he began to see the truth, just the corner of it, and it stunned him and made him ache at once, but Murali was in control now.

"You didn't have to help me," Murali said, through Miles's mouth. "It was a risk—"

"—that I took because if I hid you, it would frustrate a powerful man, which would give me power." Terris sighed sadly. "I also thought, I'm ashamed to say, that it would be fun."

"What is this?" the Lord of Dreams demanded, and without even glancing at him, Murali used Miles's hand to drive the stake into the faerie again.

"You were different," Murali said to Terris. Miles's voice was almost pleading. "You weren't like him. You helped me because you felt sorry for me. You *felt* for me!"

It was Terris that Murali fell in love with, Miles realized, dizzy. *It was Terris all along that he wanted to free. Not himself.* He laughed, quietly, in the back of his head.

Terris was right. He lied to me too. All faeries lie.

"I lied," Terris said to Murali, and Miles knew he was reading his mind, using his thoughts against Murali. "I used you, Murali. Don't paint me as your hero. I was as cruel as any faerie would be."

"But you're not like them!" Murali said, and it was a plea now. "You let him trap you."

"I didn't. I let you imagine it all. I got caught in my own trap, and I've paid. I only want to die now, Murali, and see what happens next." He reached out and stroked Miles's cheek with a ghostly finger. "Maybe next time I'll have a heart like yours, and I'll do it right."

"No," Murali wailed, and Miles felt his despair. He felt the half-fey's resolve begin to crumble.

He felt the Lord of Dreams begin to stir again.

Miles took control of his body once more and looked across the room at Harry. He was close now, watching Miles, ignoring everything else. Miles wished he knew how to free him. He wished one of the faeries would tell him, wished they would tell him more than lies. He wondered if there was any truth to what Murali said—if Miles freed him, *would* that release Harry? But no, it was Terris's spell again that bore him. The Lord truly was nothing. He was illusion only, defeated by a simple mirror. Terris was real. But Terris was just another cruel faerie, and he didn't feel—

Miles jerked his head up, eyes wide as the solution, so obvious, unrolled before him.

"No," Terris said, tersely, reading his mind again.

"You *can* feel," Miles said, ignoring him. "You couldn't before, but you can now. Or, rather, you could." He looked down into the box at the mutilated body. "You have feeling there. You just have to claim it."

"You have no idea how much that hurts!" Terris hissed, silver tears brimming in his transparent eyes.

"I do," Miles replied. "Every human does. We all face it, every day, all alone." He nodded to the Lord of Dreams, kicking like a beetle on the floor. "He gave you a gift, putting you in here. He gave you what no faerie has ever had before, no full-blooded faerie. He gave you despair, and pain, enough to move even your leaden heart. And now you *can* love Murali, just as you told him you would. You can have power you never even dreamed of—but you must pay the price, just like the rest of us. You must feel. Your body knows how, now. All you have to do is claim it."

"I will help you," Murali said, taking over Miles's body again and reaching for Terris's ghost hand. "The first part you must do alone, but once you are able, call me, and I will come to you."

"You will leave me," Terris hissed. "You're horribly fickle, and you'll leave me."

"And you'll have the power to find another, if he does," Miles said. "But I don't think he will. I've felt your heart, Terris, and now I've felt his. He does love you. He's waited as long for this as you have." Miles looked at Harry, who was watching this drama quietly, knowing how his part would end, and Miles felt heavy. "You have a chance at it that I don't. I'm going to die, because you've poisoned me. I let you, so it's my fault. I let you because I wanted to save Harry. And I have— everyone but myself." He paused. "No, that's not right. I've saved myself too. It's just that I'm not going to live to enjoy my work."

The Lord of Dreams climbed back to his feet with a feeble but angry roar. "I will not have this!"

Miles turned, and this time, it was he who took control of Murali. "See yourself," he said, and became a mirror, so that the faerie could see.

The Lord of Dreams gazed into Miles, screamed, then burst into flame. He was gone.

For a moment, Miles paused, surprised. The move had been an instinct, but while he'd hoped it would at least stun the faerie, he hadn't expected it to destroy him so completely. Especially not like that. Could it really be possible that someone who had caused so much pain to so many for so long could dissolve with just one glance at his own reflection?

He was nothing more than the reflection of the dreams of others. Which meant that he himself was nothing. For anyone else to see the Lord of Dreams, they saw their own poisonous desires and were capti- vated by them forever. But when the Lord of Dreams saw himself, he saw nothing.

And when faced with his own truth, his own reflection, his own dark truths—in the face of that, he didn't exist.

Miles turned back to Terris, who regarded him strangely.

"You're right," the faerie said. "You're not fey at all. You're something much, much worse."

"Take back your body," Miles told him. "Take it back and learn to live with pain, just like the rest of us. Take it, and Murali will get his body back, and I'll get mine." He looked sadly at Harry. "Just let me be with him as I die."

"Why?" Terris said, baffled. "What good will that do?"

"It will be one good moment," Miles said. "And it's better than nothing."

I'm sorry, Murali said, inside his head. *It was never my intention to steal your life.*

It's okay, Miles replied, and he meant it. *You didn't steal it. You gave me a real one, for the first time. Thank you.*

Terris leaned forward and kissed Miles tenderly against his lips. Then he sighed, shuddered, and slipped into his body.

Miles was aware, briefly, of a terrible scream, of a conscious being feeling real pain for the first time, beginning not as an infant but as a man, bearing it all at once and buckling like a loose strap under the strain. And he felt a course of love streak through him as Murali saw, too, the force of it wrenching him from the spell, and he was free—not for a moment, but for good.

And so was Miles.

He heard the shatter of silver all around him as it left his body, but he didn't care, didn't notice anything else at all, because as the darkness closed around him, he fell into Harry's strong arms, looking up at him blearily, blood caking his eyes as the mirrors fell away. He looked up into his lover and touched his face.

"I love you, Harry." He closed his eyes. "Even if you can't love me back, I love you."

As he slipped away he felt someone push something small and hard inside his lips, and he swallowed it. Then he drew his last breath, let it out in a shuddery rasp, and died.

And then, because the world is a funny old thing, he came right back to life.

CHAPTER TWELVE

BECAUSE AS TERRIS had told him, over and over again, it was all nothing but a dream.

Miles did not figure this out, not at first. He lay in Harry's arms, and he truly was dying, leaving in a manner that ensured he could never return. But he did not leave the mortal plane—just the faerie one.

He died an achingly beautiful death in his lover's arms. And then he opened his eyes and sat up in the middle of the storeroom floor. His neck ached, he had a splinter in his ass, and he was really fucking cold. Beyond that, bodily, he was fine.

It took his mind a little while to realize what had happened and what it meant, and so he enjoyed a few hours of shock, which he used to get dressed, fumble with his magical supplies with shaking hands, then give up entirely and head downstairs, only to start his shock all over again when he saw that no more than forty-five minutes had passed since he'd gone upstairs. He thought perhaps it had been a *day* and forty-five minutes, but when he went back to the trailer, they just looked up at him with uneasy interest and nothing more, looking mostly like they hadn't expected to see him so soon. They also looked at his hair a lot, but they didn't say anything. Not until he came closer to them, and then Julie squinted at him.

"Is something wrong with your eyes?" she asked.

Miles blinked a few times, then shook his head. He couldn't manage to say anything somehow, and Julie just shrugged and smiled an uneasy smile.

"I must be imagining things." She went back to the book she'd been reading.

Miles nodded, gruffly, and went to his room.

The computer was all in one piece. The picture frames were intact. Everything was fine. Miles stared at it all for a few minutes, frowning. Then he swooned slightly, suddenly very tired.

Maybe this *is the dream*, he thought, fumbling for his bed. *If I go to sleep, I'll wake up in the dungeon again.*

And so he slept. He dreamed of nothing, just blankness and peace. When he woke, it was morning, and he was still in his bedroom. His head hurt, and he had to pee, so he got up, worked the kink out of his shoulder, and headed down the hall toward the bathroom and flipped on the light.

His hair was pure white.

It was white. Silver-white, end to end, every strand. And as he stared in shock at his reflection, he saw that his eyes were silver too. Technically they were light gray, but when he moved, they glinted silver.

On instinct, he looked down at his right thumb, and saw an ugly gash across it, a scab forming over the top of it. Also, his ass was incredibly sore, as if he'd had the fuck of his life.

It had happened.

It had been real.

Forgetting about the bathroom, Miles turned and stalked down the hall, pausing only at his room to grab his shoes before heading out the door. He put his shoes on as he walked, then ran, laces flapping at his ankles, all the way to the forest. He ran deep inside, cutting his legs on branches and snagging his clothes, his skin reddening in the cold.

"Terris!" he shouted. "Murali!" His heart swelled, and his voice broke as he added, "Harry!" He called them over and over again.

No one answered.

He stayed there shouting until he was hoarse, and then he just kept walking, deeper and deeper into the forest until he went all the way through it and made it into a cornfield. He walked back through from a different direction, shouting even though his voice was gone, letting his heart do the calling now.

He ended up at Katie's house.

She whisked him into the living room, where she poured tea into him and wrapped him in a blanket and plied him with questions, which he couldn't answer, of course, because he'd wasted his voice shouting in the woods. So she gave him a piece of paper and a pencil.

It took him over an hour and a half to write it out, and every time he finished a page, he gave it to her. She would read it, then nod, then wait patiently for the next. After she read the first few pages, she called Julie, who came over and began reading too. Neither said anything to each other; they just read, Katie looking subdued, Julie looking sad.

Eventually, Miles finished.

I had too much silver in me. I was dying. Except I came back here. I don't understand.

"You only died in the dream world," Julie said. "Not reality."

Miles set his jaw and scribbled again. *But my hair changed! My thumb! I still feel nauseous from the silver!*

Katie shook her head, clearly as lost as he was. But Julie sighed.

"Dreams echo life," she said. "We carry some of them with us, each in different ways, but they are still not real."

Something thick and awful was forming inside Miles's chest. *But it was real,* he argued. *It happened. I felt it. I was there! You two taught me magic, and I did it! It was not just a dream!*

"Not *just*, no," Katie said, very gently. "But it was still a dream."

The thick awfulness was growing, making it hard for Miles to breathe. And see. *But Harry*, he wrote, and then couldn't write anymore.

Julie's hand closed over Miles's own. "As I said. We carry some of the parts of dreams with us."

Miles's head spun. There was a silent scream inside his head, but even if he'd had a voice, it wouldn't have come out, because what Julie was implying was too horrible for him to bear. *No*, he wanted to shout. *No, no, this can't be right!* He looked to Katie, but she was blinking hard, as if fighting off tears. *I saved him! I did it! If I get to live, I should get to live with him*, Miles wanted to cry.

No! I deserve so much better than this!

Except he knew, now, that he didn't. No one deserved anything—and even if they did, they were unlikely to get it.

He thought of Terris, looking down at his body full of pain, of his reluctance. The emptiness he knew was inside. How he had fought it. How he had sought death instead.

Death. Miles had expected death. Had wanted it, because it would be release. But it hadn't been death that waited for him, but his life. Oh, he had died, yes— the Miles who had sulked, the Miles who had raged, the Miles who could not understand that he already had a life full of goodness and worth, that he was richer and better and stronger than any dream he could ever hope to have.

He'd seen heaven, for one moment. For several of them, in fact, and all of them in Harry's arms.

And now those moments were done. It was time to live again.

Harry. The tightness overwhelmed him, pressing on him like iron bands, pushing inside him like spikes. The pain, oh God, the pain. The pain of heaven seen and taken away. A connection, known for an instant. A joy found and removed.

Miles blinked at Julie.

Smile still in place, she held her arms out to him, inviting him to her embrace.

Pain. So much pain.

So much life.

Miles blinked again. And again. And at last, with a broken sigh, he fell into Julie's arms.

He cried.

MILES SOBBED LIKE a baby in Julie's arms, wept until he was spent, but even once she had helped him back to the trailer, back to his room, even after he had slept, the pain remained. It snuck up on him at odd moments, coming up so swiftly and violently that it startled him and anyone around him, and so he learned to weep in secret, stealing away into the woods. In a way he hurt here the most, here where he so longed to see Harry or Murali or even Terris come out and tell him the joke was over, that it would, actually, be okay. But of course this never happened. And so Miles wept over and over again. He wept in his bedroom, with his face in the pillow. He wept in the shower, playing a stupid game where he pretended he wasn't crying, that it was just the water, but his eyes were always red after, and his nostrils swollen and stuffed.

His hair never changed back, and neither did his eyes. And he couldn't dye his hair, not at home or at a salon. No color would take. To be honest, he was secretly glad, even if it was just another reminder. He was glad because even though it hurt, he didn't want to forget.

He wept for his life, for all that time he had spent chasing shadows. He wept for himself, because he was afraid that he had been lost so long he would not know how to live, that he could not, not anymore.

As time passed, he *did* find the bottom of the pain, and somehow he found a way to make a place for it, and eventually he did start to find his real life again. He worked at the pawn shop, and he didn't complain, and in a way, he liked it. Part of it was because people started bringing things in for him to fix, and he did it because he might as well, and it turned out that once he stopped hating it so much, once he stopped seeing it as the sign of his decline—really, how could he fall any farther?—once that was gone, he kind of liked it. He fixed a lot of computers, but he fixed toasters too, and

TVs, and even once a wheel on a kid's wagon. He'd really enjoyed that one.

He also bought a house.

Julie and Patty had told him he didn't need to move out, but it felt right, and so he did it. He worked on the place, fixing the plumbing and stripping the wallpaper, repairing the broken floorboards and re-plastering the ceilings. The pain was back, but he knew now how to feel the pain. He had learned how to live with it.

He started making friends in Summer Hill, and yes, some of them were very strange. Not a one of them was the sort of person that Miles would have looked for in the past. But they were honest, and most importantly, they were real.

He spent a lot of time with Katie. She was still annoying and bossy and crotchety, but she melted, he discovered, when he brought her fresh baked banana bread or fixed her microwave. She was softer with him, and even a year later, she looked at his white hair and gray eyes nervously, as if he were a piece of the universe she didn't quite know what to do with. And Miles understood, so he was gentle with her, knowing it was hard to watch your illusions die around you. Because he was patient with her, she was patient with him. And it was good, in its way.

He even got along with Warren. His old nemesis had been wary of him ever since the bathroom encounter, and at first Miles had taken some joy in that. But after a while, even that didn't do anything for him.

Warren was just Warren. He'd never be a friend, no. But Miles didn't want any enemies anymore. When he saw Warren, he smiled. Warren never did relax around him completely. But he did start waving back, and he never so much as murmured a slur at him again.

There was still a hole inside Miles, though, even after a year had passed, and he began to realize that time wasn't making it any smaller. It was the place where Harry had been, where the love for the man who had helped him become himself still burned, love which in Harry's absence was pain. Miles was learning how to live with it. Someday maybe he'd find someone else to fill that part of him, but for now it was just there. It wasn't what he deserved, but life, he decided, wasn't about getting what you deserved. It was about living. It was about being who you were and appreciating what you had.

And really, he'd have been fine if that had been the end of it, and in some universe, it probably was. But something else happened instead.

ONE DAY, WHILE Miles was working at Patty and Miles's Pawn and Repair, the bell over the door jingled, and a man walked in. Miles sat behind his workbench, fiddling with a clock radio, and he glanced up briefly at the stranger and nodded before looking back down.

"Can I help you?"

"Yes," the man said, in a rough voice that was oddly familiar and yet not at all. He plunked something down on the counter. "I've come in for a repair."

Miles looked up, glanced at the item, then shook his head. "Sorry, I can't do musical instruments."

He realized what he'd just said, paused in a surreal moment, then shook his head. Nope. He was making it up. It didn't even look like the same flute, not at all.

The man sighed and leaned forward against the counter. "Miles."

Miles looked up, again, frowning because he didn't know this man who knew his name. Then he got a better look at the man, and he faltered.

Good God, but the man looked like Terris. Except it was Terris with pale skin and bad pores and beard stubble. And black hair.

You're imagining things, he scolded himself. *It's over. Don't fuck yourself up again just when you're back on track.*

"There's a music store on Main Street." Miles pushed the flute back at the man who was not Terris. "I suggest you try there."

The man's eyes darkened, and he picked up the flute, waving it threateningly. "I *will* hit you with this, you know."

"Hey." Miles frowned.

The man ignored him. He looked angry. "It was every bit as awful as I told you it would be, and I didn't enjoy it. *None* of it. It was like living in tar. And for the record, I didn't have your cuddly little lesbians to nurse me through it. It was just me, all by myself, off in some ruined corner of the universe, blubbering like a fool. It was awful, damn you."

"Who are you?" Miles asked carefully.

The man gripped the edge of the counter and leaned over it, his eyes all but shooting sparks at Miles. *"Miles Michael Larson, stop being a simpering fool and help me!"*

Patty burst through the back door of the shop, hands on her hips. "Is this guy giving you trouble, Miles?"

The man sneered at her. "Oh, please, do *try* to fine me for swearing. Because I'm just looking for an excuse to fill this damn shop with chickens. Or geese. Which poop more, do you think?"

"What?" Patty said, confused and irritated.

"Terris?" Miles whispered.

Terris turned to him and gave him a withering look. "No. It's your Uncle Edward. *Of course* it's me." He waved impatiently at the flute. "Now. Fix it, and end this, *please.*"

Miles picked up the flute, his hands trembling, the tension coming back, the silent scream rising, and he beat it all down as quickly as he could. *No. No. Don't hope. It's dangerous, and it will hurt. Don't hope. Don't. You're imagining this. You're—*

I will shove that flute, Terris said inside his head, *straight up your ass.*

Miles shut his eyes and tightened his hand around the instrument. He was glad for Patty's shouting, even glad for the geese *and* the chickens that suddenly filled the place when Patty tried to pull Terris away, because they gave him space to think. But it was dangerous, because the hope, which he had thought was carefully put away, came raging back as if it had never been beaten back at all.

If Terris was here, then Harry could be too.

It was a fracture, a fissure, a tiny spark of hope. It was a whisper that maybe Miles could be fully happy after all. That he wouldn't have to feel torn in half, that he wouldn't have to rebuild slowly, achingly putting his heart back into place, that he could have a miracle, something amazing and wonderful just like he always wanted.

But he knew, all the way down to the bottom of his shoes, that that was so much more than he deserved.

Terris sighed.

It isn't about what you deserve, he whispered to Miles, but with more tenderness than Miles remembered. *It's about what you dare to take.*

Miles swallowed hard and looked up at him. "I dared before, in Atlanta."

Terris's smile was wry. "You reached for ghosts and illusions. You reached for power, for safety. You reached for acceptance, but not of yourself. Your heart yearned, but your soul would not answer, because you only asked for dreams. Reach for something real this time. Reach for what you learned. With him." His hand closed over Miles's own. "For what you taught me to reach for too."

Blinking back a sudden blurriness in his eyes, Miles knew that even though there was no guarantee, even though he was terrified, even though he knew if it didn't work out it would open the wound all over again, he still had to try.

"Get these birds *out of here*!" Patty was shouting, so loud that she drew Julie in, too, and through it all Terris just stood there, arms folded and waiting.

Miles turned the flute over several times in his hands. "It doesn't look broken," he said at last, over the din. "It's just really tarnished."

"It's burned," Terris replied, blithely removing a chicken from the counter.

"Then how am I supposed to fix it?" Miles asked.

Terris gave him a withering look. "Not fix the flute—fix *this*! Our lives! Play it and bring them back!"

Even with the chickens and geese, the room went eerily quiet, at least for Miles.

"Back?" he echoed, his voice hoarse.

"Yes," Terris snapped. "Don't you think it's been long enough?"

"But—" Miles shook his head, his vision blurring, his chest hurting so very, very badly. "But I died—"

"You died in the dream world. In faerie. Not here. I used the pill and sent you back. But they're there, and you need to call them. They can't cross over until you bring them. Do it, Miles, and end this."

All this time? All this time, he didn't have to have

suffered? All he would have had to do was play the flute, and it would have been over?

"Why have you been gone so long?" Miles demanded.

Terris snorted. "How good have *you* felt in the past year?"

Miles didn't answer that. He just looked down at the flute, and the year fell away. All the pain was back, ready and waiting to kill him all over again.

"Why do *I* have to play it?" he asked quietly.

"Because it's you Murali chose. Because you're human. Because it's just the way it worked out. Or because he wanted to drive me crazy. All options, plus several others, are equally as likely." He waved a hand at Miles. "Play it already. Get this done."

And then Miles knew. He looked up at Terris, his heart sinking again. "You aren't sure. You don't know for certain that they can come back. You've tried it yourself, but it didn't work, and now you're just hoping I can pull a miracle out of my ass."

"Don't make this worse," Terris said tightly. "Just do it. We'll find out if I'm right soon enough."

That wasn't the answer Miles wanted. He'd wanted assurance, a guarantee. He didn't get it, and for a minute, he didn't think he could do it, couldn't play it and see, even if there was even a small chance. Better to live in pain managed than risk a chance of ending up worse than he was.

Or risk finding he could have the only thing he truly wanted.

Dreams are just illusions, he thought, fearful, and raised the flute to his lips, hands shaking. *But may I please, just once, have this one?*

There was no voice inside the flute, no whisper telling him what to play. There was no help, no hope, no guide, just a tarnished bit of silver with holes in it, which sounded frankly quite bad when he played. He tried a scale, up, and then down, and then he set the flute back down on the counter.

Nothing happened. Terris closed his eyes.

And then, like the end of a movie, like a rainbow across the sky, the door opened, and Murali and Harry walked in.

Miles thought he was dreaming. He feared he was, and his fear kept him in place, made him dig his fingers into the counter, made his knees lock and his heart pound, made him want to run even though it was Harry coming toward him, Harry with his arms held out tentatively, Harry with a sad, weary smile and tears in his eyes. Miles held himself still, afraid that this too would fade away.

Harry came around the counter, took him carefully in his arms, and it was real.

The dam Miles had gotten so used to holding up inside him burst, and he sobbed. When he lifted his head and looked into Harry's eyes, he felt the hollow place inside him begin to fill with Harry's love. And instead of aching and falling back into sorrow, he cried in joy, and he laughed, and he embraced Harry again, and kissed him.

On the other side of the counter, the same thing was happening, except Terris was more reserved, embracing Murali more elegantly, shutting his eyes and resting his forehead against his lover's shoulder, using the tips of his fingers to wipe away the bits of tears he could not stop.

Miles turned back to Harry.

"You came," Miles said, his voice shaking. "I didn't think you would. I didn't think you *could*."

"It was tricky," Harry admitted. "And sometimes unpleasant. We could not find you until someone played the flute with a pure heart. We kept waiting, and we kept hoping."

"Did you really think," Murali said, poking Terris in the chest, "that after the two of you sacrificed so much to save us, that we wouldn't turn around and do the same for you?"

"My sacrifice was unwilling and accidental," Terris said tartly, but there was a new edge to his barb, and Miles, who now understood pain very well, knew that he did not mean it, and thankfully, Murali did too.

"What," Patty said, coming back in after shoving the last of the birds out the door, "the hell is going on?"

Murali slipped an arm around Terris's waist and turned to smile handsomely at her. "Why, madam, I've come to grant you a wish."

Patty gave him a wary look. "No thank you. You're

one of those faeries. I've heard about you. I'm fine with what I've got."

Murali looked amused. He turned to Julie. "What about you, my lady?"

"Don't answer him," Patty said sharply.

But Julie stared at him, weeping silently. She looked shaken to her core, and when she was able, she shook her head. "What I long for your kind cannot give."

Murali smiled a cryptic smile. "But that's where you're wrong. I am not your usual faerie, madam, and neither is my lover." He turned and stroked the side of Terris's face. "There is almost no limit to what we can do."

Julie studied him a moment, and Terris, too. She took Patty's hand, glanced at Miles, then spoke.

"I want harmony. I want the whole world to be able to see what I see, so that it harms itself no more."

Murali laughed and shook his head. "You are as bad as Miles! But then, I should have suspected as much, because you both have the same soft heart. No, my lady. I cannot and will not grant your wish. For one, that power is not mine to grant because it is already there. The problem is that they do not wish to see it. Life is beauty, but it must be pain, too, and humans deal with that by choosing what they wish to see. However"—his eyes twinkled, and he reached for Terris's hand—"I think there's no harm in giving you a little respite from that."

He let go of Terris's hand, held up his arms, and a

soft, warm wind began to swirl around them.

"I will ask this place, this space around us, to reflect the love it sees in us, to make the invisible visible. Love is the most powerful magic of all, and there are three sets of lovers here. On the count of three, we shall all kiss, and because of the spell, we will see in this place the visual representation of the love which we have made, simply by surrendering to each other, acknowledging both the beauty and the pain."

"Are you going to make a mess?" Patty asked, crossing her arms over her chest.

"Possibly," Murali acknowledged. "But if I do, I'll clean it up. If I don't, however—if you like what you see, may I have a job?"

"Job!" Julie said, aghast.

"Him too," Murali said, pointing at Terris.

"No," Terris and Patty said in unison.

"Me, then," Harry said, placing a kiss on Miles's cheek.

"No starting early," Murali said, shaking a finger at him. He shut his eyes, then nodded. "There. It's set."

"I still don't understand what is going to happen," Patty groused.

Murali just winked at her. "Just remember, the more love there is, the better it will be. On your marks? Get set? Go!"

Miles had no idea what anyone else did, but he needed no further prompting to kiss Harry. He didn't care if the world fell down, or if nothing more than some dust kicked up—he turned to Harry and kissed him, kissed him with all the ache he had known, with all the longing, with all the sorrow, and most of all, with all the love in his heart. He let it fill him, spilling over and over until it was a river, and he kissed his lover as if the world had no beginning and no end, for in that moment, in that kiss, he knew it was true.

When he had to breathe, he lifted his head and opened his eyes—and laughed.

It was still transforming as he watched, but the room was already vastly different than the one he had been in when he started the kiss. It was no longer dull and crowded with junk but full of merchandise, good merchandise that people would actually buy, priced affordably. The tools at Miles's bench were good and strong. Not showy, just sturdy. He had shelves full of work to do still, but now Miles saw them not as bits of junk but as people's prized possessions, the tools and objects which reflected people's hearts and souls, and through Murali's spell, he could see that truth clearly.

For a moment he felt puzzled. Had anything actually changed? Were these new tools, was this new merchandise? Or was he simply seeing it with new eyes?

Some things he knew *were* new. There were vases of flowers everywhere, mostly dried, and the back storeroom was gone, turned now into a huge kitchen filled with everything Julie would ever want to bake with. The door at the back didn't lead outside anymore, either; it led to a greenhouse which was full of herbs and flowers.

"What is this?" Patty whispered, but her eyes were full of stars.

Julie wiped tears from her cheeks, but she was smiling. "Faerie magick," she whispered. Then she laughed and pulled Patty toward the trailer.

Or, rather, the space where the trailer had been.

The trailer park was still there, but it was as if it had moved over to make room for the quaint gingerbread cottage that sat at the edge of the forest, the house where Julie and Patty's car sat in the drive. It was not a fancy house: it was humble, and it needed a little work. But it was a good house, and it had a strong foundation. And there were little outbuildings, too, with a better chicken coop and a pen for goats.

Miles, heart beating faster, grabbed Harry's hand and dragged him down the street toward his own house.

It looked much the same, but there was something different about it too. It had a workshop, for starters, and there was a new car in the driveway. When he ducked inside, he saw all his own things, but he saw some other things too. He saw more books than he remembered having, and much *older* books than he remembered having. He also saw a sheaf of legal papers on a table, and a plastic driver's license with Harry's picture on it.

Harry picked it up and turned it over in his hands,

looking bemused. Then he set it back down and looked at Miles, questioning.

Miles took his hands again. "Harry—will you stay here with me?"

Harry drew Miles's hands up to his mouth and kissed them, then bent and kissed Miles in answer.

When they went back outside, Terris and Murali were inspecting a house that had cropped up in what had been an empty lot next to Miles's place. It was very pretty and looked more like it belonged in the Welsh countryside than Minnesota, but it suited the pair of them very well.

"Very nice," Terris said, sticking his hands into his pockets. "And what will we do for money, love?"

Murali waved an airy hand. "We'll sell things. Little charms, perhaps. You already have a website, after all."

Terris rolled his eyes, but he smiled too and kissed Murali on the cheek.

"How long will this last?" Miles asked Murali. He gestured to the houses and back toward the shop. "How long is the illusion good for?"

Murali waggled his eyebrows. "Ah. It's not a dream this time, Miles. This is real. It will last as long as you believe in it."

"But—but how?"

"I told you," Murali said gently, "to listen to your heart. And I warned you that dreams were not truths. All I did, Miles, was to encourage the future that waited for our true hearts to bloom before us. Your kitchen sink still drips, Miles, and will until you fix it. Julie will still be disappointed that not everyone will choose to be a vegan. But you won't struggle quite as hard to pay your mortgage payment, and she won't ever kill a chicken again or so much as touch a pound of slaughtered cow. Patty will still worry over the heat bill, but she'll be doing it so she can buy another antique, either for her showroom or for her home." He turned to Harry. "Harry will still fall a little bit in love with everyone he sees. But he'll have you there to draw him out of his fantasy and help him find an outlet for his passions." He patted Harry on the arm and leaned in close. "Might I suggest a career in fiction?"

Harry looked thoughtful.

But Miles was still having a hard time with this. "But this was magic! This was a spell! How can it be real?"

Terris lifted an eyebrow at Miles. "Oh, darling. Magic is very real."

"But—" Miles sputtered a little more, then let out a defeated sigh. "I don't understand."

Harry took his hand and squeezed it. "This is love, Miles. Our love." He looked at the houses, at the sky, at the sun, and he smiled. "This is life."

"Don't worry," Terris drawled. "I'm sure that more pain will appear eventually, if that makes you feel any better."

TERRIS WAS RIGHT. While things were very, very good for a long, long time, they were not perfect. Miles's repair business expanded into restoration, and soon he had more jobs than he knew what to do with and was forced to hire help. The garage turned into his office, and he used it to fix old chairs and tinker with antique sewing machines and yes, sometimes fix Julie's food processor. But it was good work, and he was happy with it.

It was sometimes difficult for Harry to settle into the new world, but after a while, he found his footing, and within five years, he evened out. He ran a bookshop and worried about where he was going to send his manuscript and argued with the people in the library book club about what good literature was. In short, he was very happy.

Julie's bakery business did very well indeed, so much so that she drew business from as far as Minneapolis, and eventually she opened a local organic grocery just so she could more easily order her supplies. But she still struggled with staffing and with delivery. Overall, however, she was very happy too.

Patty's antique business boomed. She always seemed to have pieces that had a story, and they were always good stories. People came from hundreds of miles away to buy from Patty because it wasn't long before the word got out that her antiques were the best. That brought her headaches too, because rival dealers would come to spy on her and try to get to key pieces before she did, but Miles knew Patty secretly loved the competition.

Murali and Terris *did* sell things: they ran a magic shop that did much better than Katie's ever had, and they filled orders from all over the world. Who did the actual shipping, Miles didn't know, because the two men spent most of their time in their garden, a garden which usually bloomed well past the frost and began blooming well before it should. In the dead of winter, they lingered in Julie's greenhouse, nursing tender buds to bloom, whispering together, and more often than not, making love.

Happy. Everyone was very, very happy.

Sometimes at night Miles would lie beside Harry and look at him in wonder, touching him, running his fingers along his lover's beard, his shoulders, and his chest. Sometimes he wondered how long it could possibly last, this love, this wonder, and this peace. Oh, Terris and Patty's fights kept things interesting, and sometimes Julie and Murali argued for weeks over a point of philosophy. And Katie hardly came over now, because somehow the beauty of the living dream Murali had created was too much for her to handle. Not everything was perfect.

But it was closer than Miles had ever dreamed.

As he lay there in the moonlight, though, sometimes he would think of the life that he had lost, of the dreams that had died to lead him to the road that had taken him here.

Life, by its definition, must contain some pain. But as Miles watched, Harry woke and smiled sleepily at him, and Miles saw what came on the other side of pain.

Love.

The love swelled within him as Harry took him into his arms. Life wasn't about what he deserved. It wasn't even about what he was given. It was, Miles knew, as he took Harry into his body, about what he made.

As the moon rose across the sky, as the faeries danced through the forest, as dreams went up from the hearts of men like prayers, Miles gave himself to pleasure in his lover's arms, then lay awake, his mind spinning not visions of fantasy but of all that he could make of his life.

About the Author

Author of over thirty novels, Midwest-native Heidi Cullinan writes positive-outcome romances for LGBT characters struggling against insurmountable odds because she believes there's no such thing as too much happy ever after. Heidi is a two-time RITA® finalist and her books have been recommended by *Library Journal, USA Today, RT Magazine,* and *Publisher's Weekly.* When Heidi isn't writing, she enjoys cooking, reading novels and manga, playing with her cats, and watching too much anime. Find out more at heidicullinan.com.

Did you enjoy this book?

If you did, please consider leaving a review online or recommending it to a friend. There's absolutely nothing that helps an author more than a reader's enthusiasm. Your word of mouth is greatly appreciated and helps me sell more books, which helps me write more books.

Other books by Heidi Cullinan

There's a lot happening with my books right now! Sign up for my **release-announcement-only newsletter** on my website to be sure you don't miss a single release or re-release.

www.heidicullinan.com/newssignup

Want the inside scoop on upcoming releases, automatic delivery of all my titles in your preferred format, with option for signed paperbacks shipped worldwide? Consider joining my Patreon. You can learn more about it on my website.

www.patreon.com/heidicullinan

THE COPPER POINT MEDICAL SERIES
Where love is just a heartbeat away
The Doctor's Secret
The Doctor's Date
The Doctor's Orders

THE ROOSEVELT SERIES
Carry the Ocean
Shelter the Sea
More titles in this series coming soon

LOVE LESSONS SERIES
Love Lessons
Frozen Heart
Fever Pitch

Lonely Hearts
Short Stay
Rebel Heart (coming soon)

THE DANCING SERIES

Dance With Me
Enjoy the Dance
Burn the Floor (coming soon)

MINNESOTA CHRISTMAS SERIES

Let It Snow
Sleigh Ride
Winter Wonderland
Santa Baby

THE CHRISTMAS TOWN SERIES

The Christmas Fling
More adventures in Logan, Minnesota coming soon

CLOCKWORK LOVE SERIES

Clockwork Heart
Clockwork Pirate (coming soon)
Clockwork Princess (coming soon)

SPECIAL DELIVERY SERIES

Special Delivery
Hooch and Cake
Double Blind
The Twelve Days of Randy
Tough Love

TUCKER SPRINGS SERIES

Second Hand (written with Marie Sexton)

Dirty Laundry

More titles in this series by other authors

SINGLE TITLES

Antisocial

A Private Gentleman

Nowhere Ranch (available in Italian)

Family Man (written with Marie Sexton)

The Devil Will Do

Hero

Miles and the Magic Flute

NONFICTION

Your A Game: Winning Promo for Genre Fiction
(written with Damon Suede)

Many titles are also available in audio and more are in production. Check the listings wherever you purchase audiobooks to see which titles are available.

www.ingramcontent.com/pod-product-compliance
Lightning Source LLC
Chambersburg PA
CBHW051842180726
48284CB00007BA/2014